Kingpin Dreams 2

Paper Boi Rari

**Lock Down Publications & Ca$h
Presents
Kingpin Dreams 2
A Novel by *Paper Boi Rari***

Paper Boi Rari

Lock Down Publications
P.O. Box 944
Stockbridge, Ga 30281

Visit our website at www.lockdownpublications.com

Cover design and layout by: **Dynasty's Cover Me**
Book interior design by: **Shawn Walker**
Edited by**: Cassandra Sims**

Stay Connected with Us!

Text **LOCKDOWN** to 22828 to stay up-to-date with new releases, sneak peaks, contests and more...

Thank you.

Submission Guideline

Submit the first three chapters of your completed manuscript to ldpsubmissions@gmail.com, subject line: Your book's title. The manuscript must be in a .doc file and sent as an attachment. Document should be in Times New Roman, double spaced and in size 12 font. Also, provide your synopsis and full contact information. If sending multiple submissions, they must each be in a separate email.

Have a story but no way to send it electronically? You can still submit to LDP/Ca$h Presents. Send in the first three chapters, written or typed, of your completed manuscript to:

LDP: Submissions Dept
P.O. Box 944
Stockbridge, Ga 30281

*DO NOT send original manuscript. Must be a duplicate. *

Provide your synopsis and a cover letter containing your full contact information.

Thanks for considering LDP and Ca$h Presents.

Dedication

This book is dedicated to all the real niggas who kept their mouths close! Shhh... No SNITCHES NO SUSPECTS! NEVER FORGET! Authentic can't be duplicated because then you would only be a copy which really makes you counterfeit. This for my real niggaz! Stand up!

Author's Notes

All I write is real shit, reachable shit, hood shit! Reality fiction man! Straight up! We gon' keep it street and keep it in the streetz! I'm penning these stories from prison in a max USP for being in the streetz and keeping it in da streetz. Look me up if you don't believe me, it's all there, homes, no cap! I played the hand I was dealt when all the spades were gone. My nigga, I'm the run down!

Much love,
Paper Boi Rari

Get at me at:
www.Facebook.com/ Levi Maddox

Or write to:

Levi Maddox-11807-002/B-Unit
Federal Correctional Complex, USPI
P.O. BOX 1033
Coleman, Florida, 33521-1033

Paper Boi Rari

ACKNOWLEDGEMENTS

I must thank God first! Much love! I'm gonna keep spreading the gossip! You already know, if y'all ain't saved then you losing, fam, real cap!

Mom Dukes, both y'all know my love runs deep. I appreciate y'all women never leaving my corner. I love y'all!

Mookie and Donnie: love y'all boyz, bra! I got y'all! Just hold on!

Dad! Whew! I did it, boy. Just when everybody gave up on me, I DID IT! Thank y'all for that, ni. Right on time! Love you, old head!!

Baby Mama: I love you! Even though you a super fuck up! I ain't gonna leave you behind like you did me. Only the strong survive! Weak always die off! I'm still where you left me at! LOL

Lady Bugg: Daddy love you, little girl! You the best!

Lil Lee: Step daddy love you. You already know!

My sisters: love y'all too! I'm here, just call!

To my fanz: Man, good looking! I fucks with y'all! I'm gonna keep 'em comin' just watch! I got y'all!

To my niggaz in the system! Man don't give up on your dreams. Only you can make it happen for you! Keep working, it's never too late. Never! Look at the Kentucky Fried Chicken man. He was in his sixties before he got right. That's why the man has the gray hair on TV for 'em, he didn't give up. Change starts with you, boy! Much love.

To my haters: LOL, don't get scared now! Yeah, y'all gonna get exposed! Everything in the dark must come to the light, like what goes up must come down! It's on, good looking!

To the snitches: Fuck you! Witness protection can't protect you, nigga! Y'all know what it is! On sight! Oh ni, Big Bear, Oozy, Squirrel, City Boy, Chico D, Blu, Shawn, Zoe, Ramsey, Mike Da Barber, T-Tone, Rod, Slimm G, NANA, PoeBoy, Bake, Big L, Alabama Shawn, Chicago D, BD, P.NUT!! Man if I forgot y'all, it's all love! I been writing so much, I'm seeing shit right now, plus my cellie complaining about the light. It's late, plus I'm on a time frame. I got to get this out in the a.m.

Much love! ALABAMA STAND UP!

Save the best for last: CA$H and the whole LDP Crew, thank y'all and much love! We the team, so let's go!

Paper Boi Rari

CHAPTER 1

TALLADEGA, AL
Federal Correction Institution

With his hands and arms crossed behind his back, Maliss paced the floor back and forth. Chopping it up with his right-hand man, Hawk, and new homie, Roe Black, the three were making plans for a big come-up.

"Man, I'm telling y'all, we 'bout to take 'dis shit to a whole 'nother planet on these folks, homes," Maliss said. "As of right now, the streets like a candy store, ya' feel me," he said, "you can get any treat you like," he said.

Maliss was waiting for his name to be called for release. He had just completed a fourteen-month Federal sentence for escaping from the Dismas Charities Halfway House, in Montgomery, Alabama, off Fleming Road.

Even though he'd killed his baby's mama, Ayesha, in his dreams, Maliss could care less if she fell off the face of the earth. She was nothing more than a carrier to him now, and she was the very reason for his incarceration. Ayesha and her new girlfriend had tried to run off with his newborn, princess Gabbie, along with his life savings of three hundred thousand dollars. So, once she found out he'd escaped, she called the law before he could get to her. She gave the authorities all the information they needed to track his moves, and it paid off too—he was charged with an additional felony, which was added to his already extensive criminal portfolio. However, since learning of his release date six months prior, she'd been begging for his forgiveness and using their daughter as leverage.

Bounce Back by Juvenile and Baby played from Hawk's Mp3 player through two pair of R-10 head phones, hooked up to a prison-made amp, customized inside a digital alarm clock. "That's real right there. Now I'm 'bout to bounce back on these niggas," Maliss said. "See, you gotta enjoy life and live like it's no tomorrow. You gotta have the business handled just in case you don't be here, man, for real. You want yo' loved ones to still be able to carry on without you," he said.

"Like what though?" Roe Black asked.

"Like real man shit, homes. You know, life insurance, for a proper burial, you feel me?" Roe Black shook his head in agreement but didn't say anything, so Maliss continued. "Like IRAs, homes."

"What's that, big bruh?"

"IRA is a tax deferred retirement account with great tax breaks, you feel me? It stands for individual retirement account. It's tax free, meaning your money grows tax free. These are things you need to know when you gettin' real bread and keepin' it. See, you gotta make yo' money work for you," Maliss said, breaking it down for him.

"I heard that sayin' before but never figured out what it meant," Roe Black admitted.

"That's why I'ma sharpen you up, bruh, 'cause you gotta be a certain caliber if I'ma make you part of our family." Maliss' face wore a serious expression.

"Now that's real," Roe Black said.

Hawk listened attentively but remained quiet. Observing had always been his first nature. He was reading the book *Jesus Calling: 365 Day Journaling Devotional*, by Sarah Young. He was getting his mental right for his day with the Lord, which was something he did every morning when he rose. At the same time, he paid close attention to Roe Black's body language and his choice of questioning to Maliss. Ever since Maliss had laced him up on the dream he'd had three days prior, his radar had been on high alert regarding Roe Black, but Roe never suspected a thing. As a child, Hawk had mastered the art of never showing his hand until he was sure it was a guaranteed win.

"I'm already hip that it's real, bruh, and that's the only way I'm comin', homes, straight facts no fiction, my nigga," Maliss replied to Roe. "See, you gotta direct and demand yo' money where you want it to go if you wanna keep it, and if you want it to grow," he added. "We invest our bread," he said, pointing to Hawk and then back at himself. "That's why we able to live as comfortable as we want to, or should I say as comfortable as these slave owners allow us to. We directed our bread to where we wanted it to go and attracted more of the same kind of prosperous friends. So they wouldn't have to do much work, they just needed to be in place, you followin'?" he asked Roe Black.

"Yeah, big bruh. I'm catchin' on," he answered. "So, when you say *invest*, how I know what to put my money in?"

"See, I know we gon' go a long ways together 'cause you not afraid to ask questions, and they legit questions too. But don't get me wrong, 'cause ain't no such thing as a dumb question if you don't know the answer. It's only dumb when you don't think to ask a question, and then ask another one if you don't understand the answer you've been given, bruh," he said.

"Them is big facts," Roe said, shaking his head up and down excitedly.

"Show you right. Now, let's lace you real fast 'cause if they don't call me in the next ten minutes, I'ma go ask Ms. Andrews' fine ass to call RCD and see what's up with the hold up," Maliss said.

"That baby sho' fine too, boy!" Roe added, curving his hand to form a crescent moon shape.

"The shortcut to knowing where to invest gon' be easy 'cause you already been accepted into the family. We gon' show you everything you need to know so that'll keep you from having to research it yo'self," Maliss told him, giving him a minute to let it all sink in. "To show you we real standup niggas, rule number one is trust no one, you dig? So, I'ma still give you the formula to do your own research just so you'll know what you've been told is right, you feel me?"

"Hell yeah, and I respect that, bruh. That's why I fucks wit' you. You gon' make sure a nigga understand the terms of any situation he get involved in," Roe Black responded sincerely.

"It's the only way, fam," Maliss said. "Understanding and communication are unbelievably valuable in life. With them two

13

resources alone, you can go to the top of the food chain, my nigga." He pointed towards the ceiling. "Before I forget though, you also need to find you a financial advisor. They gon' be the one to lace you up in the right direction. But, like I said before, and never wavier from it, trust *no one*. And even after he gives you his expertise, hit another one up until you comfortable and feel like you found the right vessel for yo' bread to run through, feel me?" Maliss asked him.

"Hell yeah, big bruh. So far, it makes logical sense to me," Roe Black said, nodding his head.

"A'ight, good. So, I said all that to say this: make sure you get yo' IRA as fully funded as you can get it, 'cause you never know when yo' last day on earth gon' be. Don't be selfish and leave yo' loved ones here to carry all the weight, fam. What if you become disabled and can't work for yo'self no more? You still got forty or fifty years of livin' left in you but no way to generate income? You'll have yo' nest egg to count on," he said. Again, he pointed to Hawk and then himself. "Me and Hawk been hip to this shit for a few years now, huh, Hawk?" he questioned, turning his focus toward Hawk.

"You already know what it is, bruh, 'cause a nigga tryna have somethin' in the end," Hawk said, speaking his first words of the morning. "It's not how you start," he said.

"It's how you end," he and Maliss concluded in unison.

"If you don't know by now, homes, you better know when it comes to the kinda lifestyle we live it's safety first and foremost, in everythang we indulge in," Hawk added. "Insurance with a capital 'I' with one hundred percent protection and return."

"Facts," Maliss cosigned. "See, me and Hawk already got a business out there right now that generates a one hundred ten percent profit rate annually. It's called *The Spot*. It's—"

"A stereo shop," Roe Black said, before Maliss could finish.

"Yeah, that's right," Maliss said.

"Damn, I didn't know y'all owned that, my nigga. That's where me and my niggas take our shit to in the 'A' 'cause we

14

know ain't nobody else in our area gon' have that same hook up and sound."

"Nigga get the fuck outta here! Don't start all that jeffin fam, I'm still gon' fuck witcha out there on the turf, Pretty Boy Floyd!" Maliss started laughing when he referred to him as the well-known bank robber. Pretty Boy Floyd had been killed in the early 1920's as the police chased him down and killed him in cold blood.

"Big bruh. Nah, for real, nigga, I don't do the flexin' so don't start doubtin' a nigga," Hawk said defensively.

"Alright. Where is it located at?" he quizzed Roe Black. "Now before you answer, make sure you correct, 'cause if you lyin' just to kick it, it'll only get you demoted with me, 'cause I consider you family. You'll lose characteristic value in this organization with the fairytale-imagination shit. And that'll only lead to all kinds of other shit that neither of us wants," Maliss said, looking him in the eyes to show his seriousness.

"Hey, big bruh, check it out right, I fucks wit' you a thousand percent, and I'm a certified G, nigga. So I know frontin' ain't gon' gain me nothin', bruh, 'cause if you fuckin' wit' me you gon' fuck wit' me regardless. I already know the kinda person you present yo'self to be. I know you would rather die than break your word," Roe Black said. "And, furthermore, homes, I'm too grown to lie to a nigga, ya feel me?" he said. "No offense or disrespect intended," he added for good measures.

"None taken," Maliss replied. Truth-be-told, if he'd felt even a hint of disrespect he wouldn't have hesitated to kill him within thirty minutes of being released—for him, disrespect by any mean's was enough to kill for.

"We waitin'," Hawk said, since Roe still hadn't answered the question.

"True that," Maliss seconded. They looked at him.

"Oh, it's in Atlanta on the North side. I forgot the name of the street but I do remember it being close to the interstate. The sign is simple. Black background with words *The Spot* in big bold letters. Do that sound 'bout right?" he asked. "Or is there another stereo place up there with the same name?" He looked from Maliss to Hawk waiting for an answer.

"Nah, nigga, that's it. But how you get turned on to us way down in Bama?" Hawk asked curiously.

"Well, I gotta cousin up there and I told him I was gon' go to Florida wit' some of my comrades to get our shit hooked up at *Beatz By The Speakers* in Tallahassee. He told me I should come up to the 'A' because he knew a place that had better prices and better quality. Said the place was called *The Spot* and that it was owned by blacks who knew how music should sound. I convinced my circle and told 'em I wasn't lettin' no redneck fuck wit' my shit no matter what they advertised." Hawk listened and couldn't help but smile, vibing off the fact that they had business coming in from everywhere. Once released, he would step his game up and start franchising *The Spot*.

"Damn, it's a small world, homes. So, did you 'preciate the work you got done?" Maliss inquired.

"What? Man, big bruh, me and my homies killin' them niggas down there. I done won fifteen bands, shuttin' shit down. I ain't gone lie, my whole lil' city tryna find out where the work came from so y'all missin' a lot of bread fuckin' with me. I was sendin' them lames straight to Tallahassee to *Beatz By The Speakers*."

"We ain't doin' no trippin'," Maliss said, as he stood up to finish the conversation. "Real fast, let me put the polishin' touches on this convo before I vamp up out of this bitch." He looked out the cell to try and judge how much time was left. Looking at his white G-Shock, he saw that the time was 7:48 a.m. "I got about 12 minutes left, huh, y'all?"

"Pretty much," Hawk said. "You 'bout to get right out and straight in the drama, huh? I know Ayesha gon' show her ass when she find out she drove all the way up here for nothin'."

"Fuck that dry-headed-ass bitch, bruh! Shit, she can afford the gas since the bitch ran off with over a quarter ticket. Bitch lucky I don't down her square ass right out there in the parkin' lot, come right back in here, fix a shot, and watch *The View*."

"'Dat's real ni," Roe Black said. "I sho' can't wait to shit on my baby mama. That's why I gotta run them bands up."

"Fuck a bitch, let's get rich," Maliss said. "And, check it out, bruh, time tickin'," he reminded him, as he reached out to dap him up. Hawk already knew what the lick read. "You got what? Eighty-eight days left before the halfway house, right?"

"You half right. I got eighty-eight days left but no halfway house. When I leave up out this bitch, I'm headed straight out."

"A'ight then, so what you tryna do? You wanna make a few more bands before you touch down or you tryna relax?" Maliss asked.

"Bruh, when have ever known me to relax? Especially when I got avenues I can take.

"Fa'sho. Say no more then. So, as soon as I get to the halfway house I'ma be in motion. I'ma set it up so you can gone 'head and run you up a Rolls truck off the land in ninety days. It's gon' be that straight panic, so make sure you wholesale that shit and stay off the scene, bruh. I'm 'bout to overdose that shit with flakka, you hear me?" Maliss said. Flakka was a popular designer drug on the streets and in the joint. "It'll be here next Monday, fact's. Pages seven, fourteen, twenty-one, and so on, until the numbers end, you feel me? I'ma send you all the fine-ass reality hoes, bruh. Let that shit go for two bands a sheet or less," he said.

"Hell if I do! Hell nah, bruh. Fuck these rat-ass niggas, man. We gotta tax 'em 'cause they would damn sho' tax us if they was in a position to do so," Roe Black spoke up.

"Ain't no doubt, but just go with the plan I already got formatted 'cause y'all are on a time frame," Maliss explained. "Puttin' tax on it gon' slow the sells down. You'll either be stuck wit' inventory, or settling for some punk-ass stamps just to end up tryna resale 'em. In this gap everything for the low, and it must go just like them signs say on the clearance racks in the stores. It all equal profits." He looked at him and paused. "You ain't got but ten days 'til yo' release, Roe. Don't come out with the same mail I sent you and an indigent account. I'm 'bout to pave the way for you to see at least fifteen bands in less than two weeks," he continued.

"A'ight, big bruh. Boi, I'm tellin' you, I need it too, and I sho' 'preciate it." Roe thanked him sincerely.

"Cut it out, man. Nigga, that ain't no bread, homes. It's just somethin' to do to keep up yo' craft," Maliss said. "My nigga, I'm about to introduce you to hundreds of millions, just stay alert and *never ever* go against the grain. I got licks set up for the next seven years, homes. I'm talkin' 'bout sophisticated, high-profile crimes. Shit, if you slip and get jammed for these kinds of acts you could get the gas chamber or ADX off top. "So, let me ask you this, you sure you can tolerate this kind of pain and pressure?"

"Man, for a million I'll assassinate President Trump, my nigga! Fuck you talkin 'bout," Roe said, his tone filled with animation. "You talkin' hundreds of mills? Hell yeah I'm ready. Why wouldn't I be? Let's get it," he said, with finality and without hesitation.

Hawk stared at Roe intensely as he tried to get a feel for him. Unfortunately, he didn't like what he was feeling on the inside about the nigga, and something just didn't feel right. But at the same time, he didn't want to question Maliss' judgement on the choice of people he chose to give an opportunity to become family. So, he made a mental note to bring it up once they were all free. He would be damned if he'd end up having to face the gas chamber on account of a generic nigga posing to be authentic. *It's too late in the game for that shit*, he thought.

Maliss looked down at his watch—the time was now 7:58 a.m. He took it off his wrist and handed it to Hawk. "It's crunch time, bruh. Let me check the door right fast." He looked out the window and saw Ms. Andrews in the office, on the phone. "That's gotta be my call, man." He turned around and looked at Roe Black. "Yo', we 'bout to eat like never before. We gon' get it out the streets but make it look like it came from the government, homes. Today's goal is for you to hit the library and do yo' research on IRAs. When you talk to me again, that's gon' be the first thing I'ma quiz you on. This how we gon' finesse free bands on these folks without touchin' our bread—our bread is for investments only. Understand?"

"Somewhat, big bruh. I will when I go do the homework on it though. I got you," Roe Black said.

"Good, that's real good, Maliss said. "A'ight, y'all, this is it. Y'all stick together like VELCRO and stay safe." He proceeded by giving them both a brotherly hug, one after the other. "Learn from yesterday, live for today, and have faith for tomorrow."

Right at that moment, Ms. Andrews opened the door. "Maleek Davis!" she called out.

"Oh now, that's me right there! Show time," he said, and grabbed his belongings.

"Bring the mat, along with your laundry, to the office and then report to R&D," Ms. Andrews directed. As she spoke, she looked Maliss in the eyes as if he were a piece of her favorite candy.

"A'ight, it's about time. Shit, after I finished lacing my men up, I thought I was gonna have to remind you it was my day. Shit, you was all up in that computer and shit like you forgot a nigga was ready to be set free," he said, dragging his mat.

"Boy, please! And, damn. You sho' was watchin' a muthafucka pretty hard, wasn't you?"

"Not really, but in my line of work it's part of the job to be aware of my surroundings, 'cause if you not, it could cost you yo' life, so to be aware is to be alive. He laughed and began to rap some bars from *Curry Jersey*, by Moneybagg Yo Ft. YG.

And I take my life way too serious
so please don't play with me
can't have that strap in certain states
but it stay wit' me."

Right on cue, she jumped in and picked up the hook:

"It got thirty shots on it like a curry Jersey."

"Fa'sho! Yeah, I see you up on that hip-hop shit too, huh? It's a lifestyle for me," he said, "so, I can relate to that shit, you feel me?"

"Mm-mm, I hear yah. Boy pick that mat up 'cause that lifestyle is what got yo' behind in here. And since you so ready to go you obviously don't like *this* lifestyle." She paused, giving her logic time to sink in then said, "Hopefully, you learned somthin' to keep you in society."

"That's your second time adressin' me as a *boy*, Ms. Andrews. Now, me and you both know that compared to all these other males in here I'm far from a *boy*." He stopped and pointed at himself before continuing. "I been handlin' manly responsibilities and situations for quite a while now. Besides that, you need to exempt that *boy* shit from yo' vocabulary, especially while you workin' inside a *man's* institution. If you like dealin' with little boys and not men, you should try to get a job at the juvenile facility," he said, politely checking her. "And for the record, fuck this cheap-ass piece-of-shit mat! I wouldn't let my dog entertain no shit like this!" He threw it down on the floor and it hit with a loud *thump*. "I'm 'bout to go and lay up on a Cali King fit for a king such as myself. Not tryna sound like I'm braggin' or nothin', but that bitch covered with a thousand-count silk Gucci sheets with the matching comforter, you feel me?" He picked the mat back up.

"I hear yah," she said. "Come on, let's get you outta here. So, what you 'bout to do to be productive so you'll be able to afford all the high-end things, you boastin' on, Mr. Davis?"

"Well, Miss Nosy, I already own, well partly own, a stereo shop in Atlanta. My partna is the young man I'm forced to leave here for ninety more days. He's in the cell I just left. It's a very prosperous, um, business," he said.

"Excuse you," she interrupted. "I'm never nosy honey, just curious to know where your head is, that's all." Once they'd made it to the door she looked at him and asked, "So, who's the lucky woman out there waitin' on you in the parkin' lot?"

"Damn, you sho' is watchin' a muthafucka pretty hard, ain't you?" He teased her, mimicking her words from moments prior. "Anyway, what makes you assume she waitin' on me, huh?"

She laughed. "Because, um, you the only one being released today, sir."

"Let me find out you one of *them*," he said.

"One of who?"

"One of them IG-followin' types." This time he was the one who laughed.

"Nigga, please. You wish." She rolled her eyes playfully.

"That's gotta be my lame-ass baby mama thinkin' she here to pick me up. Probably 'bout to cause a scene when she realize she not though!"

"What you mean? You got another bitch comin' or somethin'?" Ms. Andrews was really being nosy for real now.

"Nah, sweetie. For real though, my heart vacant right now. I'm single and independent, the best way to be, you feel me?"

"Oh, okay then." She smiled at his explanation as she unlocked the door for him. Next, she reached over and pushed a piece of paper with her number on it in his hand. "When you look at it, you'll know what to do with it." She winked flirtatiously.

"I'ma keep this piece of paper as safe as I can, but just in case you don't hear from me, when you get back to the office, get on Google and look up the number for my shop, *The Spot*. Write it down and call me sometimes. If I'm not there when you call, leave a message. Oh, and when you get off work today make sure you send me a friend request on the Book—I be on there more than any other social media site. I go by my real name so look for it under the location of ATL, GA."

As he stepped through the doorway, he looked directly in her eyes. "I look forward to seein' you on the other side, sexy. Don't keep me waitin' long either 'cause now you got me wantin' to get to know the *real* Ms. Andrews," he said.

"We'll see about that, Mr. Davis."

"Call me by my first name. I'm a free man now. Free the real!" he yelled, before heading towards R&D. "Shout out to Tee Grizzly! Fuck the rest and fuck the FEDS!"

With that said, he swaggered down the corridor, closer to freedom with every step.

Paper Boi Rari

CHAPTER 2

FRESH OUT THE FEDS
8:25 a.m.

Playing and talking to Gabbie, Ayesha sat in the car waiting for Maliss to come out of the door. Although she was a little nervous, she was never scared. Besides, the Maliss she knew would never let money or material objects come between him and the love he possessed for her and their child. No matter what she did, he would always forgive her.

"You ready to see your long-head daddy?" she asked Gabbie, as she bounced her up and down on her lap. "Huh, Princess? You ready to see da-da," she said.

"Da-da!" Gabbie said, clapping her hands together.

"Yay, da-da's babygirl!" Gabbie was seventeen months now and she could say twelve different words.

An all-white stretch Rolls-Royce Cullinan whipped in the parking lot and pulled in the space beside Ayesha. Gabbie clapped her hands and screamed at the SUV.

"Damn, that bitch clean," Ayesha said, pulling her phone out to snap a few pictures of the luxury foreign SUV.

The sounds of the electronic locks popped and clicked as the power-close, push-button front door of the vehicle buzzed open, and out stepped Maliss into the parking lot like the certified boss he was. Instead of the prison uniform he'd worn for the last fourteen months, he was now dressed in a pair of all-white YSL trousers with the white Gucci belt adorned with red G's, an all red Gucci long-sleeve button up, and a pair of red Gucci loafers on his feet. Atop his head sat a white Gucci Bucket hat with the same red G's that were displayed on the belt. The white Gucci Locs with light-red tent, and the all gold Presidential Rolex topped his look off. Gone was the casual Joe look, and he was now on his grown man shit.

When Ayesha saw him, her pussy began to jump like a heartbeat and it oozed wetness. She could hardly wait to get dicked-down with some fresh-out-of-prison, make-up sex.

"Hey, baby daddy," she said, after getting out of her car to greet him. She was smiling from ear to ear.

"Watch out lil' bitch," Maliss admonished. His arm was stretched outward, halting her attempt to hug him. Looking at his daughter he smiled. "Hey, Princess Gabbie, daddy's here, babygirl." However, Gabbie shunned him when he reached for her. "All that baby talk on the phone was a front, huh, babygirl? Daddy can't get no love?" He walked around Ayesha, so he'd be facing his daughter. Getting right in her face, he smiled and did his best to sound more animated. "Hey, daddy's girl!" This time she giggled, but when he held out his arms to take her, again, she shunned him shyly.

"Oh, I see how it is. You wanna play games wit' daddy, huh? Come to da-da," he said, and reached for her again. This time, she turned around and fell into his arms. She touched his face curiously, as recognition of who he was, seemed to set in. The familiarity brought about an instant bond between the two of them. "You comin' with da-da," he told her, before turning to walk away from Ayesha's car. When he turned around, he was met and greeted by two Asian females who had the body and looks of a model.

"Hi, Mr. Davis, I'm Lehya," the one closest to him said, "and this is Sonya." Lehya pointed toward the other female.

"Welcome home, we're here to help you adjust back into society. We're happy to be of service and your wish is our command," Sonya said.

"Nice to meet y'all!" Maliss eyed the two women from head to toe, admiring their sex appeal. Happy with what he was seeing, he smiled deviously and asked, "Any wish?"

"Any at all," Sonya replied in a low, sexy tone. Lehya returned a flirtatious smile and shook her head up and down slowly.

"Well, in that case, I'm sure I'll be needin' some roadside assistance before we reach my final destination." He licked his lips teasingly. "That won't be a problem, will it?"

"I'm sure we can handle whatever you need," Lehya said.

"We guarantee our service, satisfaction, and satisfaction only," Sonya added.

"Enough said," he replied. "So, how long will our trip take?"

"It's ninety-eight minutes from Talladega, AL to Hayneville, AL," Sonya informed him. "Once we depart from Hayneville, it'll take another hundred fifty-eight minutes, without delay, to get to Fulton Industrial in Atlanta," she said. "Without delay"—she looked at her lab top—"we'd include thirty-five more minutes, which would make the trip nine minutes short of five hours, sir." Looking up at him she added, "That doesn't include the time any *roadside assistance* in Hayneville might require, sir. Only you know how long that'll take, otherwise, I would've already had it calculated in, sir."

While Sonya was doing her numbers, Maliss stood in silence, eye fuckin' both of them. The only time he was calculating was how many times he could sex each one before arriving to their destination. He wished it were possible to do both of them at the same time. *They said anything I wished though,* he thought. "Well, ladies, I got eight hours to get there, and I paid a nice fee for an extra six hours," he said, "so, let's get ready to move out!"

Lehya stood five-four in a pair of six-inch Jimmy Choo Spring Season peep toe's. Naturally, she was just four feet eight, a midget compared to Maliss. Both she and Sonya were wearing soft-pink business mini skirts and blouses, by Fendi. Lehya was pigeon-toed with long black Asian hair that hung in soft curl's. She weighed one hundred twenty-five pounds with measurements of 39–24–42. She was a young twenty-four years in age and resembled an Asian goddess. Her ethnicity was a combination of Asian, Chinese, Japanese, and Indian. A tender dick would get a nut just from the mere sight of her.

Now Sonya, was just twenty-two years old, not much younger than Lehya. The soft-pink and black Christian Louboutin Easter edition heels accentuated her bowlegs. The black straps wrapped around them perfectly and looked like a slithering snake crawling up her calves. Standing a medium height of five feet seven inches tall, her long slender legs were tatted with Asian dragons. An even one hundred forty-two pounds, her 34-23-44 frame looked delectable draped on her popsicle waist and big donkey ass—she was super thick.

Sonya sported a pair of big pink block-shades by Gucci, and her hair was cut in a soft pink mohawk with a blue duck tail hanging from the back. An evil smiley face ring pierced her tongue, and in her nose was a small 2-carat diamond ring. Sonya was drippin' on 'em, she had the Fendi design's cut and blended on the sides of her head. Her ethnicity was a mixture of Asian, Chinese, Jamaican, Puerto Rican, and Indian. If you asked her, she'd tell you she was *Blasian*, a word she'd made up meaning Black and Asian mixed, and definitely exotic. Two gold fangs hung like the canine teeth in a Pitt's mouth. To say she was a bad bitch, would be an insult.

By now, Ayesha was pissed to the max. Even though she was the queen of fashion, always dressed for a photo shoot, Maliss could tell she was feeling a little insecure since he wasn't giving her the kind of attention he'd been giving the two model-looking Asian females. But Ayesha was a certified stack house. Standing five feet three, she weighed one hundred thirty-eight pounds without an ounce of fat. Her C-cup breasts were round, plump, perky, and bite size. Ayesha's big ass was one of her best assets, round and extra fat. She had pretty feet and she was extra bowlegged, but she was a real ghetto-fabulous hood bitch. Coincidentally, her short hair was also cut in a mohawk style, except hers was watermelon-green with a watermelon-pink duck tail. She had at least sixteen tattoos, and her eye, tongue, lip, and navel were all pierced.

Ayesha was clad in a watermelon-green dress by Philosophy di Lorenzo Serafini, assembled with a matching pink lingerie set by Fleur du Mal. Her petite feet rocked a pair of watermelon-pink spring season four-inch Christian Louboutin heel. Her hands were

Kingpin Dreams 2

occupied with rings by Renvi. Her toes and fingernails were polished in a watermelon-green Gucci design, compliments of Glamorous, a new spot out of Montgomery, AL, where the females went to get pampered. A woman's Presidential Rolex with pink diamonds flooding the bezel and face, wrapped her wrist snuggly.

Her natural scent was fragranced with a hint of *Lust* perfume created by an undisclosed name; a three fluid ounce bottle cost about four hundred dollars. Yeah, she was definitely *that* bitch, and everybody knew black overtook any color it combined with— well, usually, but not today. She could've fooled anyone but Maliss. Shit, the way he felt toward her, she could've grown a halo and wings and he still wouldn't want anything to do with her disloyal ass.

The Asians were secretly jealous of her but neither of them showed it. At the same time, they respected her taste in fashion, and it was evident, pampering herself was something she did often. The tension in the parking lot was so thick, you could've cut it with a chainsaw.

"A'ight, baby mama, I'll get wit' you in the future. I'm taking Gabbie wit' me, I'll drop her off at yo' mother house. I gotta go to the halfway house in Atlanta, but I got time to make a few stops," Maliss said, holding Gabbie tightly in his arms.

"Hell-fuckin'-nah, bitch! Give me my fuckin' daughter Maleek," Ayesha yelled. "Fuck wrong wit' you? I don't want my baby 'round no gotdamn high-end prostitutes, stupid nigga!"

"Watch yo' fuckin' mouth, Ayesha, before I break yo' jaw right out here in front of these nice young ladies. My baby 'bout to ride in luxury with her daddy. Ain't that right, Princess?" He looked at his daughter and smiled. "All you gotta do is follow me there, now don't hold me up. Let's get off these folk's property. I ain't seen or been 'round my angel in fourteen months."

"She's cute. What's her name?" Sonya asked him.

"Gabriel Leeyah Davis."

"That's a lovely name, and it fits her," Lehya said. "She has the same name as me. What a coincidence," she said, smiling at Maliss.

"Maleek, I'm not fuckin' around wit' you, so give me my baby, nigga! You got me fucked up! The fuck you thought, tryin' a bitch like that?" Ayesha said. Before anyone could respond, she reached in her car and popped the trunk.

"Y'all get in and start the truck up right now!" he ordered the Asian women.

Ayesha took off walking fast, headed to the trunk of her car. She pulled out a baseball bat and began waving it in the air as she continued giving Maliss a piece of her mind. "So, you got me drivin' all the way up here for nothin', bitch? I'm 'bout to bust all the windows out this bitch, stupid-ass nigga!" Next, she did a quick sprint over to the Rolls Royce. Maliss jumped inside the truck and quickly closed the door. However, with all the yelling and commotion going on, Gabbie began to cry hysterically.

"Everything is fine, Princess. Daddy got you, baby girl," He rocked her back and forth to calm her down. Sniffling, she lay her head on his chest and sucked on her thumb.

BOOM! BAM!

Ayesha swung the bat and hit the window closest to Maliss. Since the windows were bullet proof, the bat bounced back and flew out of her hand.

"Pull off, Lehya! We done wasted enough time on that stupid bitch," he yelled. Lehya maneuvered the big luxury SUV out of the parking lot and into traffic.

Fuming mad, Ayesha cussed and stomped as she was left alone in the parking lot. She hurried to her car in hot pursuit. "He know damn well I ain't the one to be fucked wit'! I'm 'bout to bust his bitch-ass head right at Momma's house." She continued arguing aloud as she put the petal to the metal. "If my baby wasn't in there, I would run them muthafuckas right off the muthafuckin' road!" Going well-over the speed limit, her only focus was to catch up with the limo.

WHOOP-WHOOP! WHOOP-WHOOP!

It was too late to break her speed because a state trooper had already jumped behind her 2021 Tesla Model X.

"Fuck, fuck, fuck!" She banged her hands on the steering wheel as she brought the car to a slow roll, onto the shoulder of the road. "This ain't been my damn day at all!" She took three deep breaths and said a short prayer. "God, I know I just went on one, but please get the Devil up off me, Father God. God, I need you to become my legs and walk me through this. Lead me to where You want me to go, Lord, and not where I want to go, Father God. This is Your journey, not mine. In Jesus' name and the Holy Spirit, I pray. Amen," she said, before bringing the car to a complete stop. She knew Maliss would be long gone and out of sight, if, and when, the trooper let her go.

Paper Boi Rari

CHAPTER 3

LEHYA AND SONYA
Roadside Assistance

"This bitch to die for," Maliss said, still in awe of the interior in the cabin of the Rolls-Royce Cullinan. "You can practically live in this bitch," he exclaimed. He looked around like a child during an Easter egg hunt. "Mom Dukes did it again. She know her son only want the best of the best. Don't matter what lane I fall in, it's gon' always be the high end, you feel me, Sonya?"

"Not yet, but I'm countin' on it," she said, and winked. She was seated across from Maliss with her legs wide open, savoring a chilled flute of Ace of Spades. She opened them just enough to give him a bull's-eye view to see her freshly shaved, juicy pussy. And, he could definitely see the glaze on it.

The Rolls was riding as if it was gliding on air, and the smooth ride caused little Gabbie to fall fast asleep. Maliss got up to lay her down and he could almost stand up straight inside the cabin of the luxury SUV. He grabbed a small blanket from a cabinet, laid Gabbie down on an empty seat and wrapped her up so she could nap comfortably.

"Now back to you, Sonya," he said with a crooked grin on his face. "Mom Dukes know I only enjoy the best, so now I'm sittin' here tryna figure out which one of y'all is the right one for me. Which one of you is gonna be the best *to* me, and *for* me? Or do the two of y'all together equal the best?" he asked. He looked Sonya up and down. "Both of y'all definitely look worth some of this big black, long dick. And, I can sho' fill them lil' tight pussies all the way up," he said. The thought of him stretching her walls caused Sonya's pussy to throb. "So, Sonya, which one of y'all the best in the sex department?" he asked, his tone devious yet sexy. A wide smile spread across her face.

***

Ms. Andrews was back in the office on the computer. She had already sent a friend request to Maleek's page, and she was anxious for him to log onto Facebook and see her checking for him. Her profile picture would allow him to see how she looked dressed in clothes other than her uniform. After sending the request, she also made sure to Google *The Spot* to get his business number, with plans of calling him after work. Next, she looked up the halfway house in Atlanta and wrote down the visiting hours. Since she was off on weekend she would take the risk to pay him a visit, especially since he claimed he was single. Her intentions were to test just how single he was.

While on her computer, she decided to replay the footage of Maleek on the security camera. Seeing how he'd finessed his time in lockup, and how he'd departed like the CEO of a Fortune 500 company, made her hot and horny. His drip was so hard you needed a Carnival cruise ship to ride his wave. Tired of teasing herself with the images, she got up from her desk and went to the restroom to freshen up because her panties were soaking wet.

Ms. Andrews was so geeked from the possibility of hooking up with him, she felt as though she'd popped a whole gram of pink Molly. *That's gon' be my nigga,* she thought, *and I know he gon' handle business.* "He got exactly what it takes to reach the next level in life," she said aloud, as she talked to herself on the way out of the restroom. *That's where I come in at . . . all I need to do is help him however he needs me to. Umph, umph, umph, nigga don't even know I got that come back. Once he get a taste of this good-good, he gon' be hooked fa'sho, 'cause this that straight drop.* Ms. Andrews continued daydreaming until it was time for her to clock out.

***

Extremely turned on by Maliss' boldness, Sonya couldn't contain her smile, and she still hadn't answered him.

"While you gather your thoughts, I think it's time for me to come up out these clothes and get all the way naked. But, for the record, if I have to find out the answer on my own, it's gon' be some sore pussies 'round here, and they gon' need ice packs on em' for at least forty-eight hours," he told the women.

Sonya squeezed her legs together but still couldn't contain the orgasm that escaped.

"Well, Sonya? I'm still waitin' on the answer," Maliss probed.

"Maybe I wanna choose the ice pack route and let you find out the answer on your own," Sonya answered seductively. "That way, you can decide for yourself which one of us is better, Mr. Davis. I'm no snitch, sir so I ain't doin' no tellin'."

"You sure 'bout that?" he asked. He was fully naked now, aside from the socks on his feet. He stared her in the eyes and watched her mouth get watery as it hung open in amazement.

Lehya took a peek at his package in the rearview mirror.

"Shit, if you got the rhythm to match the size, you just might be a real woman pleaser," Sonya said. "Now I understand why your baby mama had tears in her eyes. She was mad she wouldn't be getting her kitty rubbed right tonight. Too bad for her 'cause when I'm finished with it, it won't have a drop of cum left in it," she said, and licked her luscious lips. "But, to answer your question, Mr. Davis, both me and Lehya are quite masterful, that's why we're both here. I told you satisfaction guaranteed."

Sonya wiggled her finger, gesturing him over to her. "Come here, Mr. Davis. You've wasted a lot of time asking questions. "You have a delicious looking dick on you. Sit right here and enjoy some of the best *Blasian* head you'll ever have the pleasure of having in your whole life."

"Is that right?" he asked, as he got in position.

"Yeah, but don't forget your daughter is over there asleep, so keep the noises at a minimum, please," she directed him. Slowly, she slid out of her skirt and pulled her blouse off. Kneeling between Maliss' legs, she put her hands on his inner thigh and pushed them as far apart as she could. He was so hard, his dick sprang straight up in the air, and when it did, she caught it in her mouth with ease. Her mouth was so quick to grab it, it was as if she'd been bobbing for apples; except, in this case, it was more like bobbing for dick.

Maliss had already begun making fuck-faces and he hadn't even touched the pussy yet. His forehead had creases in it, and he could feel his toes starting to curl. Sonya's mouth game was on point, and she was slurping on his piece like a straight savage. Although he was right at nine inches, she was deep throating him all the way down to his nut sack simultaneously teasing it with her tongue—with no hands. Every time she'd get to the base of it, she'd slow her pace and stare up at him with intent eye contact.

Mmm . . . Slurp-slurp!

"Ahh, shit! Ahh, yeah. Umph, Umph, you got it, girl!

Slurp! Slurp!

"Oow!" he grunted out as she teased the head. At this point, he had placed both hands on the back of her head, guiding her rhythm and pace. As he brought her head all the way down on it, he'd grind upward, meeting her with his full length. Without hesitation, she accepted it like the head-master she was, with room for more if he'd had it to offer.

"Gotdamn, So-son-Sonyaa! Mmm, baby, do that shit!" Just knowing she was turning him on made her want to even better than her best work, so she began mumming as she slurped and sucked.

"I'ma f-fuck y-you to d-death- for th-this," he managed to get out.

His threat only caused her to speed up the pace and lock her jaws tighter each time she went down and up.

Slurp! Slurp! Slurp!

Maliss closed his eyes in an effort to regain control and prevent his nut from busting. He didn't want to cum yet and he knew, without a doubt, she was beyond capable of making him release before he was ready. He couldn't go out like that, especially since he had a point to prove. "Yeah bitch, suck that dick for daddy! Um-mm… You thought you was gon' make me cum, huh? Nah, bitch, daddy got too much stamina to be a minute man. Yo' jaws *and* neck gon' be achin' fuckin' wit' me, Sonya," he boasted.

Slu-rrp! Slu-rp! Slurp!

"Damn, that shit feels gooder-than-a-muthafucka, ni! Lawd!" He rambled on rumbustiously. Then, he looked up in the rearview mirror and locked eyes with Lehya. "I got somethin' for yo' pretty ass too," he assured her.

"You better have," she said.

Even though he had plans of switching the two women out, Sonya's mouth was so warm and wet, it was hard to let her stop. She was a real professional, and only an expert could lock jaws with the grip of a Pit Bull.

He pulled her up. "I'm 'bout to long stroke this pussy, ma. You already short and close built wit' yo' thick ass self. Watch this," he told her. "Since you wanna show out and spoil me with that lava head you got, I'm 'bout to show you who the boss is 'round this muthafucka." Suddenly, he paused his words as if he'd forgotten something.

"Is something wrong, Mr. Davis?" Sonya asked with her head tilted curiously to one side.

"Nah but let me make sure. Hold on for one second." He moved to third seat of the Rolls and checked on Gabbie. She was still sound asleep, so he put headphones on her and played the smooth sounds of Ronald Isley of the Isley Brothers. "That should sooth her while she sleepin' peacefully," he said, "she should be good off that. Just in case you ladies wonderin', I had to do that 'cause this time around gon' be much different. It's 'bout to get real loud and real hot up in here."

Lehya looked out the window and realized they were passing the city jail. "Well, we're in Montgomery now," she announced to Sonya and Maliss.

"Oh yeah, well, I gotta announcement to make to." Without cracking a smile, he looked from Sonya to Lehya then back to Sonya. "I'm about to plant this dick in you and it's gon' stay there 'til we get ma crib. We ain't but two minutes away. My goal is to make you have six orgasms before we hit them two minutes, plus get my first one off," he exclaimed. "I'm 'bout to tap that G-spot at *least* a hundred times."

"Don't talk about it," she said, "be about it, daddy."

"If this pussy got the right temperature and girth, it's over for you. You might even tap out." He played *Baptiize* by Future since that's what he was 'bout do. "I'm 'bout to wash away your sins for that, now come here. I want you to bend over and grab your ankles for me," he ordered. Sonya did as she was told. "Yep, just like that, just like that. I want Lehya to witness all the cum you 'bout to release on my dick 'cause she next," he told her, while staring at her ass intently. I'ma ease in you just like this, Lehya," he said, as he pushed up in Sonya.

"Goddamn, girl! Hell yeah, you da best! Shit you gripped this dick, bae, you feel me? Mmm-hum. . . Yeah, I'ma hit this with that slow, deep stroke like, umm...dis ...yess!"

"SSss . . . Mmm . . . Mmmm . . . Umm," she said, speaking in that unknown tongue good dick brings about. "Ooh, yess, fuck me harder!

"I'm on it, ain't I? Ooww, yesss, it-it . . . It's.... cummin' ni . . . Yeah!" he said, as he moved in and out, in and out.

"Cummin'!" She yelled.

"I see it! You see it, Lehya? You better cum just like this too!" he demanded.

"Let me suck it off now." Lehya nearly pleaded.

"Yes, come on, girl, 'cause I'ma 'bout to explode, please believe it!" he said, through gritted teeth. When he was just seconds away from releasing, he pulled out and Lehya was right there to catch the load. Once she'd drained him of every drop, he turned around and slid back inside Sonya.

By the time they had reached Ma Duke's place, Sonya had released eight orgasms, put her clothes back on, and was laid back on the seat in La La Land. "I ain't never been sexed like that in my whole life," she admitted.

"I already know. I could tell only a certain type of man could take you there. You need a man who can pay close attention to yo' body and make the kinda connection that can touch them hidden hotspots in a woman," he said. "You might not ever in life experience that again, unless you let me handle it. I got plenty more for y'all before we hit the ATL, long as y'all get these other three off first. Sonya yo' shit so tight shit fit like a glove. It's so good I gotta make love to you before I depart," he said, as he peeped over the seat to check on Gabbie. "This gon' be a slow deep penetration. I'ma have your leg's in the crook of my arms, and we gon' be chest to chest, eye to eye, wit' me holding you on the edge of the seat, talkin' to you 'bout how good you makin' me feel. You gon' cum so hard in this position. I'ma be goin' so deep in you like this, and I can control the moments to accomplish this for us, you feel me?"

Sonya shook her head as she lay curled up on the seat in a fetal position. Maliss had really worked her over and she was feeling it, but she knew she needed to recuperate so she could perform again when the time came.

"I see you over there wit' yo' eyes closed," he said. "I'ma always leave you wit' yo' pussy throbbin, baby."

Paper Boi Rari

CHAPTER 4

HAYNEVILLE, AL
Ma

The Rolls Royce finally pulled up in front of Ayesha's mother's house and came to a stop. Her mother had been looking out of the window, waiting on their arrival. Upon seeing the white stretch, she walked out on the porch to greet her son-in-law. Lehya stepped out and opened the door for Maleek so he could make a grand impression.

His mother-in-law, Mama D, didn't contain the frown on her face until she saw Maleek step out holding Gabbie in his arm.

"Oh baby, I didn't know who was about to get out of this truck." She lied. Ayesha had already called her crying, and she'd told her mother what happened in the prison parking lot. "You pulled up ridin' like you the president," she said, and laughed.

He was smiled. "What's up, Mama?" He bent down and hugged her neck with his free arm.

"Ain't much happenin' 'round here 'cept the same ol' same ol', Maleek. Just workin' hard and providin' for these kids, tryna get them some of what they ask for," she told him. " I see you still doin' pretty damn good for yourself. You stepped out in style, huh?"

"Come on, Mama, you know I wouldn't have it no other way."

"Yeah, I know you make a way when it ain't no way. That's one thang I always said about you, now. I hope you plannin' on stayin' out here, Maleek. "You see this lil' girl right here?" She pointed toward Gabbie. "She gonna need you around. You a real man and they don't come like you no more, Son. I'ma always love you no matter what you and Ayesha go though, you understand me?" She asked with a serious expression on her face.

"I know, Ma, and I love you for that, and you know I'm here for you whenever you need me." His tone matched the seriousness she'd displayed seconds prior.

"So, what you 'bout to do with yourself now that you out?"

"Well, while I was locked up, I decided to further my education in the business field, so I'm 'bout to shape the environment to my personality so I can give back to my people, Ma. And give this little princess everything she asks for," he added. He kissed Gabbie on her forehead lovingly. "That's part of my plan," he said.

"Oh, okay. Sounds like you got it all figured out, huh? Umph, Ayesha gonna be lookin' real crazy when she see you out here doing yo' thang without her, ain't she?" Mama D chuckled.

"You already know, Ma, but she made her own bed. It's over right here though. I ain't fuckin' wit' her no more I'm gon' for real this time."

"You back down here or you still in the big city?" Mama D asked.

"I'm still in the city, Ma. Matter of fact, I'm on my way there right now. I gotta go to the halfway house, but I just wanted to see you before I went." He dug in his pocket and pulled out his prepaid debit card and gave it to her.

"Thank you, Maleek, boy you always been good to me," she exclaimed sincerely.

"Stop playin', Ma, you know how we do," he told her. It's seven thousand on there, that's for you."

"That's part of why I love you the way I do, Maleek. Be safe and stay out of trouble, you hear."

"Thanks, and I love you too, always and forever. But let me get goin' before yo' crazy daughter pull up." He half joked. "I know she had already called you to let you know I was bringin' Gabbie."

"Yeah, she did," she said, smiling.

"Wake up, Gabbie. Daddy gotta go babygirl," he said, gently shaking Gabbie in his arms. She opened her eyes and yawned as she stretched. "Daddy love you, okay." He kissed her on her each cheek and then on her forehead before handing her over to her grandmother. He hugged her once more and she wrapped her little arms around his neck returning the gesture. "That's right, daddy's girl. Give daddy some love." He kissed her on her cheek one last time and waved goodbye as he turned to leave.

She waved back. "Tah-tah, da da," Gabbie said.

Maleek jumped in the whip and Lehya got in with him. Sonya closed the door behind them and jumped in the driver's seat and took off. "The time?" he asked.

"Well, we were actually ahead of schedule by eight minutes, and we've been here twenty minutes. So, ninety plus twenty is a hundred and ten, which is an hour and fifty minutes. That leaves us six hours and ten minutes," Lehya said, looking at the time on the laptop.

He clapped his hands together and looked at Lehya with a devious smile on his face. Returning a smile of her own, she knew what time it was, specifically since she'd been anxiously waiting to get in the ring and perform.

As they pulled off Ma's road and turned onto the highway, they passed Ayesha. As soon as she saw them, she rolled her window down and stuck her middle finger out at them, while holding hard on the horn.

"Good timing," Sonya said, looking in the rearview mirror at Maleek.

"Yeah, I been mastered the art of timing, so take heed and always be aware of it," he said.

Paper Boi Rari

CHAPTER 5

BACK ON THE ROAD

"We got plenty of time so let's just enjoy the ride," Maliss said. "When we get to Montgomery stop by the Walmart on the Blvd. I need to pick up a few things to take in wit' me," he said.

"A'ight, I gotcha. Hold on a sec, I'm 'bout to turn the music down right quick," Sonya said. "Go to Walmart on Blvd." She spoke into the GPS.

"Walmart located on South Blvd. We will be arriving in twenty-eight minutes," the automated GPS voice announced through the speaker of the SUV.

Lehya pulled her blouse off, exposing her pretty titties which stood up firm and perky. "It's my turn to get some me-time before we make this pit stop." She stood up to take off her skirt.

"Nah, leave the skirt on, just take off whatever you got on under it,"

"The only thing under this skirt is Miss Kitty," she said.

"Put that stick to da model's back on," Maliss told her.

Lehya pulled his dick out and began sucking on it greedily with her hot, watery mouth.

SLURP! SLURP!

"Umm," she moaned, while bobbing her head up and down with on his massive dick. In a matter of seconds, she'd made it stand to its fullest potential. She was giving him the kind of blow job that made his mouth ball up.

"Shit." He let out a moan and reclined the seat so far back, his feet were in the air and his head almost touched the floor.

Lehya got up and slowly and sat on his face. She grinded up against it and with powerful sucks, she leaned over to retrieve his dick between her lips.

She slow-necked him as her body trembled from the climax she was receiving due to his experienced tongue game. He was most definitely blessing her game room.

When she popped him out of her mouth, her mouth released a loud *POP!* She began slapping his dick on her tongue as she teased the head. He wrapped his arms around her waist and proceeded to tongue-fuck her, while using his fingers to tease her button. Lehya released him. Unable to form words with her mouth, she proceeded to make sex faces and inaudible noises. Her hands rested on his legs and a slight hump formed in her back, as her body went up and down, riding his face as if she was performing a lap dance.

Maliss was in his own world, and he had zoned out on her clit. She let out a loud growl. Her heels were planted on the floor and she moved like a Hawaiian-dance girl. Biting down on her bottom lip, her eyes rolled back in her head. "I'm cummin' again," she screamed.

He pushed his finger back inside her. "Cum for me," he coached her, "right here on my tongue, Lehya."

He blew on her opening. "Cum for me then," he said again, before sucking on her love button.

"Ooh, I'm cumin'," she moaned out, as she bucked and jerked, "ahh, yes, yes!"

He sopped her up before she put his dick back in her mouth and sucked with force. His toes curled up so tight, they looked like fists. "Just like that," he said. "Yes, girl." He licked the rim of her asshole really slow.

"Mmm," She hummed around his dick and tightened her jaws and throat. She turned her head sideways, bobbing all the way down, coming all the way up to the tip, with perfect rhythm.

"I'm 'bout to nut, Lehya!"

"Pulling into Walmart's parking lot, less than one minute," the automated GPS announced.

"Yes, just like that! Don't stop, ooh you bet not stop!" he shouted, as he arched his back upward going down her throat.

Maliss licked her rim slowly, while she continued to drain him of his last few drops. "Ahh, shit," he groaned.

Still sucking the head, pulling back 'til her jaws touched, she was showing out and putting on for her city, When she licked his pee hole and slowly eased down the full length of his pole, her nose touched his nut sack. Lehya swallowed up every drop, greedily She pulled up on his manhood while clenching her jaw muscles tightly and slowly. She wanted to milk him dry and leave him completely empty.

As she and Maliss breathed heavily, he sat up and wiped his mouth with the back of his hand. "Whew, you worked a nigga out!" he said, looking at her in amazement. He was thoroughly satisfied.

"I had to go in on you since you blessed me with that fire-ass head. It was only right that I return the favor," she said. "You gotta have strong will power and a focused mind to go with all that stamina. A bitch can't slip wit' you or she done 'cause your sex game is to die for," Lehya told him. She looked at him. "I see what's going on now. You might just be the last of your kind, Boo, straight up," she said, finally laboring her breathing.

Maliss listened with a crooked grin on his face, and he knew he had hooked them both. Lehya and Sonya had no idea, the sexcapade they were on was part of a bigger plan. He knew exactly what he was doing, and he didn't mind using himself as a pawn, especially since both women were fine as hell and extremely easy on the eyes. They were now officially *his* bitches, and he would state his claim before getting to the halfway house. He had instructions for them to follow and rules they couldn't break. The *double r's* is what he liked to refer to them as, which stood for *rules and regulations*.

"Lehya, you just fucked me up for real! That's all I'ma say. Y'all come on, I'm 'bout to run in here real fast and grab a few things. That was road side assistances part two, when we get back, road side assistance part three coming out illegal activities."

"Nole!" They both said. At the same time.

"You off the chain," Sonya said.

"Grrr," he growled at them and made an evil face. "If y'all satisfied with what you already experienced, this last scene gon' be considered a bonus feature that ain't never been seen before. So, be advised," he said. "I don't recommend y'all try these demonstrations unless you been properly trained or supervised. These positions are tailored made and designed especially by me. Anything seen is at the viewer's discretion, ya' heard," he said, with a serious face expression.

The ladies laughed out loud.

"Mr. Davis, you are something serious," Sonya said.

"Yeah, think it's a game if you want to," he replied.

"Shit, I can't wait to be graced with that dick. I ain't had my turn yet," Lehya said. "Fuck all that shit you talkin.'"

"Don't trip, I gotcha. Since you talkin' like that, you up first. Before you try somethin' you think you can handle, I should let you know I been known to put females in comas."

"Yeah a'ight, I'ma slam dunk that dick into this ocean," she said.

"A'ight, that's the body of water I love to drown in. Y'all need to get somethin' to eat too so y'all can be energized for the next demo. I'ma grab a few things too 'cause y'all just went the fuck off on a nigga! I'm fresh out. Ain't I blessed?" he asked, boasting on being surrounded by two beauties.

As they exited the Rolls truck, all eyes were on them. All three were dripping like a pot of grandmama's chili. They appeared to be business-like people that any average person would love to meet. They moved with purpose, and a strong sense of power. Each one mirrored the others' swagger which made their shine shimmer even more. Maliss was a real boss-type nigga, so the confidence he exuded was natural for him. To have top notch women on his arm's was like wearing long sleeves in the winter, normal.

Lehya and Sonya were used to being in the company of powerful people, so the looks they were receiving were looks they'd become accustomed to. However, there was something different about Maliss, he had touched on their emotions, something they weren't used to. As the two women sauntered to the entrance on the store, they made sure to put on extra hard for him, and with class.

Once inside, Maliss went straight to the hardware department. "Y'all meet me at Mc Donald's in ten minutes," he said, before sending them on their way. In the meantime, he grabbed the item's he needed for the halfway house and part three to their demo. He grabbed some zip ties, a few more disclosed items, and a bottle of KY. Next, he went inside Verizon and purchased the iPhone X with a phone card. After he'd picked up all that he needed, he made his way over to the McDonalds and grabbed a number 4 with an extra pickle.

"I see y'all got them bellies full, huh?" he asked, smiling at Lehya and Sonya.

"Yep, and ready to get something else full too," Lehya said.

"I know that's right, girl," Sonya said.

"Bet that up," Maliss said. "Let me fuel up so I can make that happen."

Thirty minutes later, they were pulling back into traffic with cool five hours left to bullshit.

Paper Boi Rari

CHAPTER 6

ROAD SIDE ASSISTANCE
Illegal Activities

Sonya had taken her place back in the driver's seat to allow Lehya to get her juice box tapped. Now, everyone was silent in their own place of thought. Maliss was taking advantage of the time, getting his phone activated. He needed to call Mom Dukes since she was the one keeping *The Spot* functional while he'd been away. He had moved her down to the 'A' from Detroit, MI. While there, she'd fallen in love with the south, especially the weather, in comparison to the Midwest. She also loved the people because they were more social and friendly.

"If you don't mind me asking while we're in recess, what were you in the Feds for?" Lehya asked.

"Escape," he said. Looking at his phone.

"Escape from where?"

"The halfway house."

"Get the fuck outta here. And they tryin' you again?"

"Yeah, but this ain't the same one I escaped from—that one was in Montgomery, Alabama."

"Oh, well, why you leave?" She probed further.

"BM was playin' some dangerous financial games and family tricks with a nigga."

"So that's why you ain't fuckin' with her?"

"Facts!" he answered nonchalantly.

"What are you 'bout to do in life now then?"

"Shit, I got a whole portfolio of stuff to do."

"What's the first and main one?" Lehya continued.

"I'ma 'bout to bring out a house whole name with a chain line of businesses under it."

"Okay, sound's good. What's it called?"

"Illegal Activity."

"Catchy! What's gon' be the first business?"

"Well," he said and took a deep breath, "I got a pattern for my line of sex toys and costumes. I wanna introduce that first 'cause it'll be the most affordable to fund, feel me?"

"For real? You came up wit' all this by yourself?" she asked.

"You can't tell?"

"Well, you do have a high sex drive but that don't mean I should automatically assume anything about the topic in and of itself."

"True. But, yeah, it's all my idea. The ideas came to me in a dream and I realized it was a gift sent from God. He was showin' me how to be able to provide for myself, and my family, the *right* way. By being on the straight and narrow, people will love me instead of hate me," Maliss said sincerely.

"I like that, and I look forward to supportin' you. Everyone knows sex is important. And it sells," she said.

"Most definitely, and that's why it's my primary goal. When it comes to sex, there's much that needs to be uncovered 'cause society has shied away from all that needs to be seen heard, and explained about sex. And they don't speak on it," Maliss said. "They leave it up to the individual to wanna know more. If a man or woman don't do the research for themself, they'll end up being the average kind of sex partner who's satisfied with the basics of intercourse," he added. "We're in a world where people believe and learn from what they can see, and not what they can't, ya' feel me? So, if they don't see it, they most likely won't look for it either, so I'm 'bout to keep it in their faces. You know what I'm talkin' 'bout?" He rubbed his chin.

"Yeah, you gon' definitely go far, so go for it. Sounds like you got your shit together so you gon' be a'ight," Lehya said in response.

"Once we finish up our sexual festivities, I'ma present somethin' to y'all before we depart," Maliss said.

"We all ears!" Lehya smiled.

"I'm listenin'," Sonya chimed in. She had joined them in the back.

Making sure the women didn't see him, Maliss reached inside the Walmart bag and pulled out the black FN BB gun. He pulled out the zip tie's and three pair of stockings.

SLURP! SLURP!

Lehya pulled Maliss' dick out and proceeded to give him some professional head. Once she brought him to his full length, she stood up and stripped butt naked, leaving nothing on except her heels. She unbuckled his belt and pants and yanked them off of him.

"You in a hurry ain't you?" he asked, as he lifted himself to help her out.

"Um-mm. You takin' your time so I guess I gotta take the dick." She climb up and squatted down on top of him and pushed the button on the side of the bucket seat. She reclined the seat back until she was satisfied with the angle. "I'm about to ride that dick like I did that tongue . . . nice and slow," she said. She straddled him and grabbed his dick with one hand while placing her free hand on his chest. She made sure to keep direct eye contact as she guided him inside her. "Sss," she moaned as she eased down slowly.

His mouth opened and he bit down on his bottom lip. "Damn, you super tight," he said, gritting his teeth from the feel of the stimulation.

"Umm," Lehya moaned as she slowly eased herself all the way down on him.

With his hands wrapped firmly around her waist, Maliss caught her off guard and pulled her down hard and fast. He did an upward-thrust while arching his hips at the same time..

"Ahh," she screamed out. She sat still for a moment as she allowed him to fit snuggly inside her. She felt herself loosen as her juices oozed down on him. Placing her hands on his shoulders for leverage, she wound her hips and ass real slow, back and forth.

"That's right, just like that . . . nice and slow," he said. Looking in her eyes, he held her in place and bounced her and down roughly.

"Oh, Sss." She moaned in bliss.

"Um-mm, I'ma tear yo' lil' short, fine ass up! You like that, huh?" he asked in a demanding tone. He lay his back flat on the seat.

"Lay right there, baby, and let me ride that tongue for a minute," Sonya said. With one knee on each side of the headrest, she placed her hand on the ceiling for support and climbed up on his face. "Keep riding that dick, Lehya, we got his ass now. Tag team baby!" She had put the Rolls Royce on auto pilot to drive itself so she could get in on the action.

"What took you so long?" he asked. She dropped down on his mouth without further explanation. She was too turned on to talk at the moment. He licked her wetness. "Um-shit," Sonya moaned. She held one hand on the ceiling the other on his head, as if she was straddling a bull in a rodeo.

Lehya continued to ride slowly and proceeded to lean up and lick Sonya's rim. The three were having a full-no orgy-fest and they were going crazy.

"I-I'm cu-cummin'!" Sonya screamed at the top of her lungs,

Since Maliss was trying to hold out for his last demo, he made sure to control himself as to not release. He had to do it to pull it off, but afterwards, it would be a wrap. Cop, lock, and block was how he did it every time. He'd cop 'em, lock 'em in, and then blocked anything and anybody who tried to distract them. Judging from the looks on their faces and their body reactions, he knew he'd achieved his intended goal—just like he always did. A person had to be highly gifted to operate multiple position's at once. There was a format to becoming a successful boss, and Maliss understood that concept well. He realized everyone had, at least, *one* talent. He also understood that some people may not have been aware of what their talent really was, so those were ones who would try anything instead of embracing what came naturally, and perfecting it.

He had studied the facts of astrology—why humans acted a certain way, what influence the stars and planets played in peoples affairs according to the positions they were in before they were born. Things like which zodiac related best with another, and so on. All he needed to get a better understanding of a person was their birth date, month, and sometimes the exact time that person was born. With that info, he possessed a power that would be hard to reckon with. To operate his team successfully, he would place his people in a position so their zodiac signs explained what their most gifted attributions would most likely be. In order to reach a female's heart, you first had to stimulate her mind, and that's exactly what he was doing to Lehya and Sonya.

He had set up the entire encounter with the Asian women before being released from Talladega, FCI. He'd used his *hitter*, the name given to cell phones that had been snuck inside prisons, to look up the Escort Limo services on the web in Talladega, FCI. Everyone at the Talladega, FCI had hitters so looking up the service hadn't been an issue. Every female employed at the service had a profile which included her zodiac sign; coincidentally, they were all either Libras, Capricorns, Geminis, or Scorpios.

He knew he needed a Gemini because they were super smart in a wide range of subjects, meaning they could multitask. This was where Sonya came in at. She would be more versatile, true to a Gemini's nature. He chose Lehya because she was a Scorpio. Scorpios were known to be vicious, unforgivable, and overprotective lovers. She was going to trick all kinds of people if he had anything to do with it. She had the kind of long hair that added to her sophisticated business-look. Her sting was deadly and he knew she'd be a perfect fit for his plan.

Finesse was an art. It was his way of life and he always had to exercise it to keep it strong. He was finessing *the art of seduction,* to obtain the *free bands* the world had to offer.

Sonya got down and he made Lehya get up. He pulled out the zip ties and stockings first, and checked to see if the new iPhone he'd bought was fully charged—it was.

"We 'bout to do a lil' role playin' ladies then we gon' go 'head and wrap this session up, and kick it for the remainder of the ride," he said. "I'm about to demonstrate another part of my business that I'll be expandin' in the near future."

"Okay, whatever you want, Mr. Davis," Lehya said.

"Um-mm. What she said." Sonya concurred.

"A'ight, but y'all please call me Maleek from here on out," he said. "Check it out though, these are for bondage." He held his hand out and showed them the zip tie's. "And these"—he paused— "are for gagging." He showed them stockings.

"OK," Sonya said.

Lehya remained silent, anticipating what he was going to say next. Most importantly, she wanted to know the roles she and Sonya would play. When he pulled out the FN BB gun, her pussy began to jump and juices streamed down her legs because she was secretly in love with guns and danger.

"The brand is called *Illegal Activity*, so everything gon' be based on crime, and porn is gonna be the lane I swerve in. We gonna make a bootleg now, but this one is gon' be for our own enjoyment, but if she pop off right, I might wanna leak it. If I do, I'll be sure to get y'all's consent before I make any more copies," he said. Maliss had an aura about himself that made the women trust him instantly.

"This gonna be a robbery scene so y'all put your clothes back on. Once the camera is on, I'ma freestyle the rest, so be natural 'cause we want it to seem as real as possible, okay?"

"Alright," Lehya said, as she pulled on her skirt.

"Okay," Sonya said. She stood and made her way to the front of the SUV so she could check on the auto pilot.

Once everyone was dressed, he set his phone up in the position he thought to have the best angle. He allowed the women to set their phones up in angles different from his. With all the different angles, they'd have multiple captures to exchange and choose from.

Adjusting his dreads, he pulled the stockings over his head and down his face. "Lehya, you sit right here. Be natural and pretend to be talkin' about some big dope transactions you overheard your boyfriend talkin' 'bout and how much money he got stashed away. Sonya, you act like you doin' her hair." He set the cameras.

"Okay," Lehya said.

"Gotcha," Sonya said, and took her place.

"A'ight, y'all ready?" he asked. "In one, two, and action!" he said. Each camera came on, one second behind the other.

"Girl, you know Stacks and Que ain't comin' home no time soon 'cause I overheard him talkin' about meetin' up wit' a new plug Stacks met in Miami" Lehya said, as she played with her fingernails.

"Shit, fuck it then, we might as well go on a shoppin' spree compliments of them. I just stashed a lot of bread for Que and I know you put some change up too, girl," Sonya said.

"Que gon' beat that ass if you touch his gwap," Lehya joked.

"Yeah right. That nigga know." Sonya laughed.

"Bitch, put yo' muthafuckin' hands up and don't nobody move or it's gonna be brain matter all over the floor and walls!" Maliss said, as she came from the front of the SUV. He made it look as if he'd just entered the vehicle.

"Please, don't hurt us," they said.

"Shut the fuck up, bitch! Scream a fuckin' gain if you want to!" He held the gun in Lehya's face and pressed it against her forehead.

"OK, OK, what do you want? Just tell us," she said.

"Where that fuckin' bread at?" he asked.

"We ain't got no fuckin' money," Sonya said, mean mugging him.

"Oh, y'all don't? Get the fuck up, bitch, and hurry the fuck up!" He helped her point the gun at Lehya. "Get over there and put your fuckin' hands around the seat and bend that ass over," he told her. "You," he said to Sonya, "tie your hands up, bitch!" Lehya was now in a doggy-style position leaning against the seat. "Now you come get over here and climb over her and hook your arms under hers, and hurry the fuck up," he ordered them. Sonya did as she was told and straddled Lehya like a jockey.

"No, please don't hurt us. There's nothin' here," Sonya said, looking back at him.

"What the fuck I say do, bitch?" Maliss shouted through clenched teeth. He grabbed her throat and placed the gun to her temple.

"OK, OK, I'm doing it," Sonya replied. "Just promise you won't hurt us." She hiked her ass up allowing her pussy to peak out. Next, she bent over, hooking her arms through Lehya's.

He tied her hands with the zip tie's before gagging them both with the stocking's. "Since you don't know where the money at, I'll just have to settle for the money makers y'all were born with," he said. He took his clothes off and pulled out the pack of Gucci condoms his mom had put in his wallet. Both Sonya and Lehya frowned, wondering why he'd suddenly decided to use condoms since he hadn't used one earlier. He rolled the condom on the FN barrel. "I'm about to blow them pussies away," he announced. The women seem to get turned on from the anticipation. The only thing they could see was one of the phone's he had behind them as they lifted their skirt up.

POW!

He smacked the shit out of Lehya's ass so hard, she hollered and jumped at the same time. She attempted to cry out, but the sounds were muffled.

He rammed the barrel of the FN in Sonya's pussy. "Mmm," she moaned.

He switched up and began plunging the pistol in and out of Sonya. Just as they were passing through Lagrange, GA, he rolled on one of the Gucci Condoms. "Have y'all ever been fucked in these pretty fat asses before?"

The two women muffled out incoherent sounds.

"I'll take that as a yes."

He grabbed the KY jelly and lubed them both up. "NO? Is that a *no* I hear? I'm about to kill these lil' virgin asses. Yeah, you first midget!" He rubbed Lehya's fat ass with lube until he was satisfied. "Look at how wide and juicy yo lil' midget ass is." He climb over her and worked his dick in until he had loosened her up. He used Sonya's shoulders as leverage and began fucking Lehya's ass hard and fast. Her face turned a bright red. "This ass good and tight," he said. "So, you gon' tell me where the money at, huh?" he asked as he continued digging her back out.

"Mmm, mm." She let out more muffled moans.

56

He snatched the condom off and replaced it with another one. "Your turn now, Sonya." He rubbed her soft ass then eased in. He fucked both of them in their asses repeatedly before fucking their pussies to a pulp. When he was done let them suck off until he released all over their faces.

"Yeah, I'm keepin' y'all for myself," he said, as he untied them and let them get cleaned up.

By the time they reached Fulton Industrial, he had laced them on his vision and where they could be in eighteen months of dealing with him. They agreed to the terms and programmed their numbers in his phone.

"Thank you for that wonderful experience, Maleek. It was wonderful," Lehya said, shaking her head from side to side. "Too bad we can't kidnap your ass and take you with us. You got us all fucked up in the head and now—" She stopped talking and decided to just leave it at that.

"I really enjoyed y'all ladies. For real. I fucks wit' y'all now 'cause that's how a nigga supposed to get out and wing back into the community, on the real! That took the edge off a nigga," he said, smiling at them.

"Yeah, but now you have to go in there and we won't be able to get to you when we want to. Fuck the halfway house," Lehya said.

"This shit is just temporary, bae. I'll be on home confinement in less than a month," he told them both. "I already got a job so just be patience. We gon' be good." He knew Lehya had a temper and was very possessive because that was the Scorpio in her.

"Okay, bae." She poked her bottom lip out as if she was pouting.

"Be safe and we'll see you soon, baby," Sonya said, just before they pulled into the halfway house parking lot.

"Very soon, and I'ma for sure fuck with y'all. You belong to me now, so don't trip," he said. "But, let me get on in here 'cause y'all got a nigga feelin' exhausted. I must admit, I ain't never did that much work in one day. Y'all turned me on so much, I ain't want it to end," he said. "Shit, I was tryna get it all in one day now my dick sore. I'm 'bout to go take a shower and crash. Hell, a nigga might not wake up tomorrow!" They all shared a laugh. Sonya and Lehya were tired as well so they planned to take the rest of the day off to rest up. "Fuck wit' you ladies later," he said, and exited the Rolls Royce like the boss he was.

After making his way up to the entrance of the halfway house, he pressed the button on the door and waited to be buzzed in. As he thought back on the ride over, he smiled in admiration of the work he'd put in.

To finesse you got to be blessed! Thank you, Father God! I know You love me 'cause I believe and trust what I can't see, but know it's there for a fact, he thought. *All faith. Amen.*

CLICK!

The door unlock and he walked in with fifteen minutes to spare. It was Monday, April 7, 2020, his first day out the Feds.

CHAPTER 7

MS. ANDREWS

It was Monday afternoon, April 7, and the time was 3:47 p.m. It was Ms. Andrews' favorite part of the day, and her relief was there to take her place. She was more than ready to go home. She hated her job because the prisoners were so disrespectful when it came to the women workers. She was ready to quit her lame ass job since the only thing she liked was the benefits it offered. Other than that, working for the government was some cold shit.

Today, she was even more enthused to get home though. She couldn't wait to follow up on Maleek Davis. She had called *The Spot* and left her information just like he had asked her to do. She had also sent him a friend request, but she was going to follow up anyway.

Ms. Andrews was considered a top notch bitch in the prison. She kept up with the latest trend and stayed flyy. She invested her pay check on herself, kept the latest hair dos, and wore the latest name brands. She had all the retro Jordan's and LeBron James' kicks. Her nails stayed done with the most present designs. She'd gotten a set of veneers that gave her a Colgate smile. The next thing on her agenda was to get her breasts and ass done, even though she knew she was as bad as any of those reality bitches. However, in these days and times, it was just the thing to do.

She was five feet six and weighed one hundred fifty-eight pounds, with measurements of 39-24-46. Her skin was the complexion of caramel and mocha blended together. Her self-esteem was as equally high as her confidence, and she considered herself a diva.

The prisoners knocked on the cell windows as she walked down the sidewalk towards the administration building, headed to her ride.

"Ole' nasty, perverted-ass nigga," she said. "I gotta hurry up and find me somethin' else. I can't keep tolerating these fuck niggas! Hell nah," She mumbled as she continued walking by, never looking back. The knocks kept coming and got louder and louder. "Desperate and determined, damn! Don't nobody wanna see they little nasty dicks!" She knew they were jacking off on her. She pulled her coat down trying to hide all the ass she had, but it slid its way back up. Finally, she stuck her middle finger up.

She made her way to her car without looking back and didn't bother to speak to any of her co-workers either. She wasn't there to make friends, just money. She drove a green 2019 model LT Camaro. "Finally," she said in raised tone, as she turned her phone on and started her car.

She had texts coming in back to back but none of them appeared to be from Maleek. *He probably hasn't gotten his phone yet. I'm sure he'll hit me when he gets it.* She was confident he would call her. She looked at the text but didn't open any of them because she didn't see any that looked unfamiliar. "I ain't trippin' though. I'll just hit up *The Spot* again after I get home and take me a relaxing bath," she said. "I'ma see his ass soon anyway," she said aloud, as she drove home.

***

She got home and left her number at The Spot a second time, this time with a message for him to call her ASAP. Afterwards, she took her a long hot bath and went to sleep, thinking of Maleek.

That night, she dreamed that she and Maleek were in Hawaii making love under a waterfall and running. They played on the beach while he chased her in her bikini bottoms. Awaking her from her sleep, the alarm clock went off and she'd usually turn it off on Friday nights since she was off some Saturdays, but she'd forgot. She reached over and hit it off. "Umph, yep, that's exactly how we gonna be," she mumbled as a wide smile spread across her face.

It had been a long week but she'd made it through. Saturday was finally here and she was ready to see Maleek Davis. She made sure she was sexy to death from head to toe. She wore a powder-blue spaghetti-strapped body dress made by Fendi and it hugged every curve she'd been born with. A pair of Easter-pink Manolo Blahnik heels wrapped up her thick calves like a snake on its prey. Her feet were slightly exposed, showing of her toenails which were colored in a shade of powder-blue. Her long hair hung down her back, bouncy and shining, compliments of *Malaysian*. Her skin was flawless so makeup wasn't needed.

She looked in her long mirror before leaving. "Yes, hunni, you killin' these bitches as usual," she said, and blew a kiss at her reflection. After making her exit, she was en route to Atlanta, GA.

Paper Boi Rari

CHAPTER 8

Maliss was in the bathroom inside one of the stalls, responding to an email from Roe Black. He had ducked off since there was zero tolerance for TracFones, cameras, and internet. He read the email again before responding to it:

> RB: Oh ni Maliss, good lookin bruh! dat bitch Porsha lookin too good. Everybody love that bitch boi! dey kickin out top notch for her. U know she get a stack ah better. Itz luv homes. Ima hit u up in a few. Shit. 2 and a wake up baby! Monkey town here I come! Later bruh!

Black had ended the text with a smiley-face emoji. That was the first mistake he'd made—talking reckless via email bout sensitive information. It could've been a mistake and he thought he was being discrete, or maybe he just didn't give a fuck, one way or the other. Maliss had overlooked the error when he usually would've caught it. It was definitely a mistake that would cost him a healthy price later down the line. He texted Black back after rereading the email:

> M: Time is limitless, it waits for no man. As people we always plan for the future and forget about the present. You gotta conquer dat first in order to be prepared for da future Roe Black. Money is time. Master it. You good bruh. I told u Ima fuck witcha tha long way bruh. One!

After sending his response, he got on the internet and ordered a variety of drones. He needed to do some spying on a few situations to get ahead in the game, and doing it from above was the smartest move. He pressed the numbers on the TracFone's keypad and entered his prepaid debit card number to have the drones delivered overnight to *The Spot*.

Another text came through his phone and it from Lehya.

> L: Whats up Maleek? How u doin? If u need anything hit me up I gotcha bae.

He texted back:

> Maleek: I'm good just chillin. I'm cool rite now, good to hear from u. Hopefully I be on home confinement one day next week after I pay my 25%. Life is great!

As soon as he pressed the send icon another text chimed in, this time from Sonya, so of course, he opened it and read it:

> Boss: Hey Bae, how life treating u? Can't wait to link up again, Ms. Kitty drippin & soak n wet for u!

Again, he smiled and texted back:

> S: I'll see u soon Sonya, life is grand Im in my best moment's. TTYL.

He got up and stuck his phone down in his the little pocket on his Gucci boxer briefs then headed toward the TV room to watch the morning news on HLN. It was 9:35 a.m. so he was already dressed since he had to go out and work from 11:30 a.m.–5:00 p.m. Working was how newly released inmates gained free time away from the halfway house.

He needed to get to his laptop and look on the dark web because his dog, Asian T, had put him on to some shit while he'd been in the joint.

Today he was Gucci down again. He had on a black Gucci Tee with the big midnight blue colored G's and midnight-blue Gucci shorts with the matching Gucci Belt. On his feet were a pair of black Gucci slip-ons with the blue G's, and he'd worn a black Gucci bucket hat also with blue G's. He hid his eyes behind a pair of black Gucci shades retro, the Biggy Small edition. Everything had come fresh off a Dapper Don mannequin.

As soon as H.L.N. came on an employee from the halfway house stuck her head inside the TV room. "Mr. Davis? You have visitor," Ms. Harris said.

Maliss frowned because he hadn't been expecting anyone. I wonder who the hell is, he thought, as he stood from his chair to go find out.

Ms. Andrews was standing there looking good as a muthafucker, and she knew she was killing shit. Everyone stared as if she was a celebrity or someone of high caliber, but she paid it no mind. She didn't care about anyone's opinion except Maleek's. She could feel the butterflies in her stomach while waited.

Maliss bent the corner gliding in his slip-ons, dapping hard like he had the FN on him. He stopped abruptly the moment his eyes landed on her. Ms. Andrews smiled hard at the sight of him. *Damn, he look good as hell*, she thought, licking her lips. He had received her message from his mom, but he'd put it on the back burner. He hadn't hit her up yet on purpose, but he was getting around to it. He walked up on her still holding the frown on his face which made her uncomfortable.

"Hi, Maleek. I hope this isn't bad timing, 'cause I can leave. I was up here in the area so I decided to stop by and see you," she said, lying nervously.

Silently, he stared in her eyes trying to read her motives. Then without warning, the biggest smile spread across his face as he went in for a hug. She felt so soft in his arms. "Nah, you good, just surprised to see you so soon, Ms. Andrews." He released her from his grip and stepped back to take in the sight of her.

"It's VerAysha!"

"A'ight, VerAysha. So, what brings you this way? Because I don't remember you sayin' you was comin' this way this weekend. Or I would have asked you to stop by."

"You brought me here Maleek. I can't even lie," she admitted.

"How?"

"Because, I wanted to surprise you, and when you didn't respond to any of my messages, I needed to see you face to face to find out what the problem was. I'm not the one to be ignored, Maleek, so don't play. But, that's why I'm here."

"Hold up now, you better not be one of them stalkin' type females. I ain't wit' that crazy ass shit right there now."

"Nigga please! I ain't got time to be stalkin' no nigga. Look at me," she told him, and waved her hands in front of her body like one of the *Price is Right* showcase models.

The two sat down and enjoyed the rest of the visit. They decided to make plans to see one another in the near future. After the visit came to an end, he left for work.

CHAPTER 9

J-Racks had received a disturbing email from his brother, Red Dog, who'd been keeping tabs on Maliss for him. Maliss had been released which meant there was a strong possibility his money could slow up. J-Racks was a bonified hustler with long arms in the game, and the game had been good to him. He had survived many ups and downs, but a lot of niggas his age couldn't say the same. Since Maliss had been subtracted from the streets, Racks had started adjusting to the newest market of designer drugs. He'd grabbed a plug out of Montgomery, AL., from a youngster off the South Side, who went by the name Slick Nick.

Slick Nick was selling them to him for seven dollars per fifteen-gram pack. In turn, J-Racks would then sell them for twenty-five dollars a pack. The problem was, Slick Nick couldn't supply J-Racks' appetite, at least, not how he wanted and needed. He couldn't direct him to a better plug either, or maybe, he just didn't want to lose J-Racks' clientele.

Slick Nick could only provide him fifteen hundred packs at a time. J-Rack would have the shit gone in forty-eight hours. So, it was too much back-and-forth traffic for a person of his caliber. In order for Slick Nick to fulfill the demand he really required, he'd need to cop, at least, twenty thousand packs at once, for an estimated price of one dollar fifty, to two dollars even.

Now that Maliss had been released from prison, he was worried about losing the little bit of product he'd been getting. He knew Maliss would come out like the socket because everyone would plug him. Somehow or another, he'd managed to keep up with the latest drugs on the street, and he knew what the customers and fiends wanted. Even behind bars, he was always able to keep a plug, J-Racks just couldn't understand how.

Little did he know, Maliss had never been a dope boy at all, in fact, he was a certified 'Jack Boy' who could manipulate any situation that involved major bread. He was a people person, and for one reason or another, they always seemed to flock to him. Not only did he possess the gift of gab, but he knew how to finesse any situation, regardless of what it entailed. Whatever the customers wanted, suggested, or demanded, he was going to supply it in large amounts until it played out.

J-Racks was clueless to the fact that Maliss was the reason Slick Nick had fucked with him in the first place. See, Slick Nick was Maliss' little GD brother from the South Side of murder town and he'd sent Slick Nick to Foxy Lady in Columbus, GA. to specifically run into J-Racks—a game plan to get some bread until he got out. Then, he'd be able to supply him whatever he asked for, and when it was all said and done, he'd take all the shit from J-Racks.

***

Slick Nick had just made it to Sin City and over to the Walmart off the 280 Bypass. "I'm pulling in now, bruh," he said into the phone.

"A'ight, I'm parked by the flower and trees section in the back," J-Racks answered.

"Bet." Slick hung up and drove to the back, parked, and got out to greet J-Racks. "What's up wit' it, Ol' Skool," he said, as he hopped in the car with Racks. He had a book bag in his hand which he used to help shield the GLOCK 40 in his waistband.

"Same ol' same ol', young blood. Tryna buy somebody out, you feel me? So, keep yo' ear to the streets, so I can put some real bread in yo' pockets for you, homes."

"Man, shit 'bout to change. Matter of fact, I got somethin' in play as of right now," Slick said. "I met somebody who said they could get me whatever I want as long as the bread right, feel me?" he asked. He rubbed his chin knowingly.

"I *am* money, youngsta, fuck you mean?" J-Rack hit his chest for emphasis. "I'll back you on that part, you just make sure it's gas and the price is official, that's all," he said, hitting his fist in the palm of his hand. He was becoming excited feeling as though his luck was about to change.

"Yeah, homes, I'm talkin' 'bout flavors like Bling Bling, AK-47, F&N, Bob Marley, Future. Gold Rush, Pink Panther, Darth Vader, and that Hulk, nigga," he said, running down some of the most wanted drugs on the streets. "And all of that shit is top-of-the-line grade. Mufuckas gon' need super vision to smoke that shit," he said, boasting.

"Oh, hell yeah, I like the sound of that now. What's up with them numbers though? 'Cause for real, bruh, I don't usually spend no more than six figures and don't re-up no more than twice a year, lil' homes."

"Well, like I said, homes say he can provide whatever I need and he done locked it in wit' me. The more I buy, the cheaper the price gon' be. Shit, wit' you talkin' numbers like that"—Slick Nick paused for a split second—"I gotta get 'em for at least a bill a piece, my nigga. Let me do some negotiatin' and see what's what. We don't wanna speculate, plus I got my own bread too now! I'm tryna invest 'bout seventy-five bands to a bill twenty-five myself now, OG," he said. He poured it on really thick just like Maliss had laced him up to do.

"Shit, youngin', you talkin' 'bout some money, huh?" J-Racks was shocked to hear he had so much money to spend. In in his opinion, most young hustlers were usually just talk and more in the way than anything. All they wanted was a nice whip with some cheap rims, an expensive pair of kicks, and they were good to go. "Shit, if you got paper like that to invest back in the trade, you doin' damn good," he said. "Most of these niggas I know been out here grindin' they whole life and ain't never seen 30 grand at one time. How old you say you is again?" He looked at Slick Nick curiously.

"I'm twenty-three, OG. And most young niggas don't understand the value of a dolla 'cause they don't understand the concept behind this shit," he said, repeating things he'd heard Maliss say. "That's why they stay stagnate instead of elevatin' in the game, OG. They only in it for the fame of it.

These niggas nowadays ain't tryna have shit, don't know how to have shit, and ain't gon' never have shit!" He clapped his hands together to stress his point. "They have no goal's in life. As long as they can get a pair of J's, a chain, some rims on a whip with no real value, fuck 'em a few thots, and do 'em a few mid-level drugs, man, they cool. You feel me?" Slick Nick was a different bread. He was an alpha male in his generation, and he was trying to pave a way.

"Come on youngsta, you know I feel you. I been in this shit way before you was even thought of." J-Racks looked at him seriously. "I got everything a man could ever wish for. I got kids by bitches you only seen on TV. I got Rolexes older than you, homes." He chuckled. "This my city, Slick. I own it, and I been runnin' this bitch with a iron fist for a long time." He wasn't lying either. "I hustle 'cause I love to do it, man. It's my passion, and it's crazy that I got all this shit and still in the field, right?" he asked.

Slick shook his head in the affirmative, so J-Racks continued. "Yeah, I know, and wit' the luck I done had, I should'a been stopped, my nigga. I was in the game, coppin' dope at the same level as Big Meechie and them, bruh." He shook his head. "I just love the adrenaline this shit give me. Once them boys got jammed up, and they got Craig, and EL Chapo, it was a wrap the 'caine tip, for real, feel me?" He hunched his shoulders. "The new wave kicked in with the ice and Molly, plus the pills, and now the drug game."

He continued to drop jewels on him. "Remember this, you only as good as your plug allow you to be, feel me?" He let it sink in then continued. "If I can find a supplier on this new wave like Chapo had, I'ma run this shit up the elevator, youngsta. You talkin' and dealin' with a multimillionaire and don't even know it. I like you though 'cause you got a old soul." He stopped and allowed Slick to gather his thoughts.

"Yeah, that's what they tell me, OG," Slick said.

"So what do you got in mind to do wit' this game? How you gone capitalize from this lifestyle before it throws you a curve ball and strikes you out, youngsta?" he asked, wanting to see how far ahead the young dealer really was.

"I'ma let you know when you done talkin', OG. Right now, I'm tryna learn from you, but when you finished schoolin' me I gotcha. So, carry on," he said.

J-Racks smirked at him. He respected his mannerism. He nodded his head and began to speak again. "A'ight, respect, respect. See this ten thousand five hundred dollars I'ma 'bout to spend wit' you? It ain't nothin' but a *Bally* coat for me, no bullshit. I spend this kinda money on recreation and clothes. Once I really feel like I'm on top of this new wave I'll start dishin' out some major cash and support my community comfortably," he said.

"What you mean by *comfortably, OG?*"

"I mean, they just want to alter their minds and ease some of the struggles they face every day. They wanna spend money safely, and they depend on me to do that for 'em, youngsta," he said. "I been holdin' them down for over thirty somethin' years now so they depend on me for that. To be real wit' you, that's what I thrive off of and live for. It's my duty, and that's why I never quit on 'em," he said.

"Oh, I can feel that. A store they enjoy shoppin' at," Slick Nick said, pointing towards the Walmart shopping center. "They know what they gon' get every time they come!" He nodded his head.

"Right, and I can show you how. Show you how to retire, son. I beat the FEDS when they came for Meechie them then I slid out of that city and came back to my home town," he said. "I put my bread in this city and got the community all the way back behind me. They got everything they need in Sin City except them good drugs they lookin' for. I'm gon' say this to you and then I wanna know your plan before we make this transaction and get the fuck outta here. I know I just burned your ears the fuck up, didn't I?" J-Racks asked, smiling.

Slick Nick started laughing. "Nah, OG, you good. I got a pair of lungs too. We still got a little time," he said.

"I know what it take to find the shit, now don't get it twisted and slip on me," he said, "but, truth be told, I'm too rich to have to do that, and I'm too old too. So, *no* I ain't got the nerves it take to hit that interstate no more, Son," he said. "That's why your bread gotta be right. So, it can be yo' power and work for you, Slick Nick. I been Kingpin status forever now. I can help fulfill yo' *Kingpin Dreams*, just stay down till you come up. Now let me hear what you got," he said. He leaned back in his seat and prepared to listen attentively.

Slick Nick looked at J-Racks through a different set of eyes after all the wisdom he'd just volunteered to share with him. He had no idea he'd been involved with such a powerful man. He'd been serving J-Racks for six months straight, but this was the first time they'd opened up to one another. In the beginning, he just assumed J-Racks was an Ol' Skool trying to make a dollar to feed himself. Now, he could see why Maliss was keeping eyes on him. The nigga was a genius and he'd been *that* nigga all along—the fucking Nicky Barns of the south, a muthafuckin' Kingpin in the flesh. Now, Slick Nick felt even more obliged to assist Maliss with his endeavors, and he would carry them out according to the plan. He knew Maliss would bless him copiously in the end, and that was a *kingpin's dream*.

"Well, OG. See, this just a avenue for me to generate enough bread to be able to take care of me and my family until I can put up enough bread to invest in the business I'm tryna open up," he said. "This way, I can save without havin' to give my investors more leverage over me than I care to share, feel me?"

"I'm listenin', youngsta," J-Racks said.

"I want at least fifty-one percent or more ownership of my business plan when I present to these people, OG. So, man, I ain't entertainin' no lame ass bitches right now. I don't care 'bout no cheap ass cars whose value will depreciate before the ink even dries on the paper. I'm tryna own my own, OG," he said. "I wanna open up somethin' so the kids can have somethin' to look forward to. At the same time, I want them to be able to have fun while learnin' things that's gonna be beneficial to them, now, and in the future, OG," he added.

"Sound's good so far" J-Racks said. He pulled out a blunt and emptied it preparing it to fill it with Kush.

"Straight up, man, the kids are the future, and they need to know it and be showed it, and always be reminded of it," he said. "We supposed to be the ones teachin' them their worth and responsibilities so they'll be able to grasp control of their environment instead of fallin' victim to it." Slick meant every word he'd said. He looked over at J-Racks lighting up the Kush.

"Yeah, I hear that, youngin'. So what you gon' call yo' business?" J-Racks asked, as he hit the blunt a few times.

"*It's Fun*, OG. Yeah, that's gon' be the name," Slick Nick said, and nodded his head. "The concept is for them to exercise physically, along with being challenged mentally, but all the while, they still get to enjoy they self too. They'll get to win prizes as a reward for the will power they put forth. That way, they learn what it is to wanna accomplish a task all the way through, without giving up and feelin' defeated, OG," he said, as he accepted the blunt from J-Racks.

"So, in order for me to build an establishment of such wit' the vision I have for it, I'ma need at least half a ticket or better to put down on it. It's my vision, and nobody ain't gonna be able to run it like me but me, 'cause I know how, and what it needs to function. I also want to franchise it within three to five years," he said. Slick hit the blunt a few more times and passed it back to J-Racks. "See, this needs to be international too," he said, as the Kush kicked in and begin to relax them.

By now, people were passing by glancing at them. They were probably getting a whiff of the aroma seeping through the crack of the window, but that didn't deter the two from conversing and puffing.

"Kids everywhere will enjoy and appreciate this. I'm here to change, or should I say help, bring change to the world as a whole. I estimate my efforts to save one thousand children out of every three to five thousand. With that being said, this why I really get it out the mud, OG." Slick reached for the blunt again and J-Racks obliged him. Taking a deep toke, he held it in, released it slowly, and continued elaborating on his dream. "My nigga, I'm collectin' every dollar I can off the ones who wanna waste their lives and stay high, with no purpose in life. I'ma help them invest their money, by investin' it into the little ones who ain't old enough to understand the opportunities of the world. I'm helpin' the people who ain't wise enough to invest, or don't care enough to invest, make sure the generation under them is able to keep our beautiful world afloat and together, bruh." He was good and high now so he was going in. "I'm not out here playin', homes."

"Shit, I see," J-Racks said. He was high as hell too. He was fanning his right ear, but Slick didn't catch on. J-Racks was just fucking around with him anyway, so he stopped and let him continue.

"Once I get this shit in motion, I'ma be able to sit back and reap the benefits of it all. We gon' be able to go down as one of the greats people gon' remember and 'preciate, OG, real cap," he said. Taking the blunt back, it was about a quarter from being gone. "That's what I do it for. I got these investors see, and once they see my vision and get to doin' the numbers, they become greedy and try to get more control than me. They wanna rob you of yo' own fuckin' idea and put *they* spin on it. Make it operate how *they* see fit, now that they understand the concept, you feel me, OG," he said. "That's why I'm comin' in the game on top. I'ma have this shit all on TV with eliminations and big giveaways, OG. I just really wanted to let you know you ain't dealin' with no underage shit. I'm way advanced, a alpha male of my generation," Slick Nick said, flicking the roach out of the window. "For real, I don't even fuck wit' niggas up my way unless they older than me, wit' some fruitful jewels for a young brotha like myself. If not, I'm dolo. Niggas don't mean you no good. They just around to see what they can get from you. With that said, OG, I'ma try to spend so I can pop correct numbers and we can move on," Slick Nick said. J-Racks had started fanning his ear again. "Roll the window down if you hot, OG." Slick's eyes were low and heavy, and he still hadn't caught on.

Kingpin Dreams 2

"Hell nah, I ain't hot, nigga!" Racks laughed out loud. "I thought I could talk a nigga's ear off, but you just burnt my shit up, nigga!" They both burst out laughing, both high as hell. "Nah, for real, I'm bullshittin', Slick, but you gon' go along ways in life with that mind frame, little homie. I love the vision 'cause kids are the future." He took a second. "The world gon' love you for the help you provide to the kids. You helpin' 'em get where they need to be in life and keepin' 'em off these streets."

"I know, OG," he said, as he watched a bad redbone walk by and enter the store.

"You got to have somethin for 'em when they become teenagers too. They can become distracted and lose momentum. Once you start, it's gon' be your duty. You got me wantin' to invest 'cause I know it's gon' pop! When you get everything ready to go, let me know, I got a 'M' to invest on it, just make sure my return is correct, lil' nigga. Other than that, I'm in," J-Racks said. "Far as the number goes, I want twenty to fifty thousand packs at sixty-five cents a pack. Deliver it to the door, I'll pay two dollars fifty cents, Slick.

Since you put the shit together and based on the insight you just gave me, I got a bonus for yo' ass too. A hundred and fifty thousand plus on every pack, and you get the fifty cents on the two dollars too," he said. "Now *that's* fuckin' with you, Slick. I want all the flavors you called out, and I'm ready as soon as you are. Hit me up ASAP and let me know what the lick read, you feel me. Fuck with that SBA.com and they'll direct you in yo' business and lead you the right way," Racks said.

"Fa'sho, I got you. I'ma be on the same pattern we been on. I'll brief you in forty-eight hours and let you know what the status is. If it ain't broke, why fix it? Shit, same place, same time," Slick Nick said. He dapped him up and finished up the initial deal.

They made the swap and followed the same routine as always, straight to the crib, no stops. They had both gained a mutual respect for one another. J-Racks was digging his style, he liked his purpose and could tell he was on his grown-man shit. Slick Nick respected the longevity J-Racks had and the success he had been able to maintain. He'd kept an iron fist throughout three decades and hadn't been jaded once. That was unheard of these days, unless you worked with the law, or had gotten out of the game.

These days, all the streets wanted was synthetics, since it wouldn't show up in the urine tests at the good jobs they wanted to keep, especially since the whole state was seemingly on probation. Everyone wanted and needed their bills paid, so they needed to maintain their freedom, yet still have the benefit of getting high in their free time.

Your name held weight if you were getting down, if not, like everyone else, you were simply a victim of that almighty concrete jungle. No one could escape it if they stayed in the game too long. If the concrete jungle didn't get you, I'd be damned if the Jack Boys were going to let a nigga enjoy all the bread without settling out, and that's exactly where Maliss came in. It was called: 'fattening the goose before you pluck him'.

Maliss had waited a long time before he went after J-Racks. He was a well-known Kingpin who had to be finessed right. He was back to inflict pain one city at a time, or all at once if he could manage it. He was coming for the free bands, and he would flood the city by putting his people in the right positions to control the turfs. First, he had to get J-Racks out of the way.

J-Racks was right about the city being his, but see, that's where Slick Nick came in. No one knew him there and J-Racks would shelter him from everyone. He would be the only one in the city with the merchandise, that's why he'd only met him at Walmart.

"Right on fuckin' time to juice this shit up before Maliss come through fuckin' shit up," J-Racks said to himself, as he made his way to his destination. "I'ma have to get his bitch ass whacked. If he come through now, he gon' have to cop from me for a change, and I'ma charge his ass the max." He was feeling himself and the smile on his face showed it. But, little did he know, shit was about to get bad, and everything that glittered wasn't gold.

CHAPTER 10

MONTGOMERY, AL HALFWAY HOUSE
Roe Black

Roe Black had made it to the halfway house, and he'd been able to make a few bands to take along with him. His lil' bitch from the 'A' had picked him up and took him there.

She was a cute light skinned, thick hood chick who had moved to the 'A' and she'd had a crush on Roe Black since childhood. After picking him up, she'd spent a few racks on him to get him the things he'd be needing while he was there.

"A'ight, bae, good lookin' for the love, for real though," Roe Black said.

"Ain't shit to it, luv, I told you I had you. I'm in a good position now and I'm doing me. No kids, got two jobs, you know? I'm just tryna get ahead and have somethin', while enjoyin' myself at the same time. That's what it's about in the end," Shyray said. "Havin' somethin' in the end when it counts, and ownin' some shit, bae. Then when you leave this world, you can leave somethin' for ones you love when it's time to pass it on. Shit, what else could you ask for, you feel me?"

"I hear ya', Shyray. I see you on top of yo' shit," he said.

"If you know like I know, you would get yo' mind right and get the fuck out this country. You need to come fuck wit' me up in the muthafuckin' black mecca, nigga," she told him, looking him up and down. "Instead of tryna convince yo'self you somethin' you not, 'cause ain't nobody thinkin' about yo' ass down there," she said.

"Why ain't they? They love me, girl. What you talkin' about?" he asked.

"If they loved you so much, they would be here right now and woulda been wit' you from the beginnin'. You shouldn't have to convince somebody to fuck wit' you. No matter what the situation is they gon' be there regardless if they really fuck wit' you, shit. I see though, you gon' take yo' dumb ass right back down there and try it again, huh? You gon' prove you that same stupid dope boy you always said you was, huh?" she said sarcastically.

Roe Black was known for trying to be a high-end dope boy but he really didn't understand the true concept of hustling. He had never made it beyond two ounces of ready rock. He was always trying to follow, and out do, the H.T.H.G. niggas. The H.T.H.G. was a group of hustlers known as the Hill Top Hustler Gang. They'd had the city on lock in Troy, AL. until they all caught conspiracy charges, and got separated and dispensed throughout the FEDS. They would always be remembered and respected as neighborhood ghetto super stars because most of them were still in the chain gang.

Roe didn't want to go with her because he didn't know what to do with her. She was too pretty and way too much for him. He knew he wouldn't be able to control and guide her in the right direction. He was used to average females because his confidence was stronger when they were average. He could run over them while they chased him, allowing him to do whatever he wanted, without consequences behind his actions.

"Nah, but I got my plans together. Plus, my kids down here, Shyray. I can't just leave 'em like that," he said, looking at her as if she'd lost her mind.

"Boy, who you think you foolin'? You ain't thinkin' 'bout them kids. I can't vouch for what it feels like to be a father, and neither can you," she said. "I hate I had to say it like that but it's true and you know it is. This ain't yo' journey, boo, it's God's. You gon' perish if you think otherwise and try to follow your own road," she said. She stopped talking and looked at him long and hard. "Oh, I see . . . you wanna be the next Lil' Hook, huh?" She shook her head. "Umph, umph, umph, so you gonna let a diva like me walk out of yo' life? Let me find out I'm way too bad for you and you really scared for real. Well, at least I got to feel the dick this time," she said flirtatiously. "Muah," she said for emphasis, as she kissed him on the corner of the lips.

"I respect and understand everything you just said, Shyray. But, I'ma have to pass on the offer to go with you, bae. I love you," Roe Black said. "It's just not our time yet. You got yo' mind on whatever it is you tryna do, just like I got mine on what I'm tryna do. It's not about who's right or wrong, love," he said, holding her by her hips. "It's just somethin' I can't explain, but what's meant to be will be, bae. Thank you for everything you've done for me, real cap. Make sure you drive safe on that road, and I'll be checkin' in on you," he said.

He knew she had touched on some real facts about his old life, but he didn't feel like trying to explain his plans to her. He knew going to black mecca wasn't in his plans. Right now, baby mama season was the farthest thing from his mind, and he didn't necessarily have a period of when it would be. Nevertheless, she was right in a sense. There were quite a few people he wanted to see him shine—mainly, the ones who didn't want to trust him with more than an ounce at a time, and the ones who had hindered his potential to grow in the game. The ones who didn't want to see him have anything most definitely needed see him come up.

"Rosheed, be safe and do the right thing 'cause them kids need their daddy. Those are little girls, Sheed," Shyray said. Then she reached in and gave him a warm hug.

"Make sure you hit me up sometimes, Shyray, for real," Roe told her and squeezed her ass firmly.

"A'ight, I love you, Sheed," she said, as she stared into his eye's.

"Love you too," he replied. "I got the kids so don't worry 'bout that. You drive safe, bae, you hear me? I'ma gone get in here before they come looking for me." He laughed and kissed her again before getting out of the car. He watched her pull off, and then he turned to go inside the halfway house.

***

See, Lil' Hook was bred with street smarts and common sense. He had a unique gift when it came to flipping birds—he was the reason his team could run through bricks with the skill of brick masons. For young black men their age, they enjoyed extravagant lifestyles, and Lil' Hook had become a millionaire by the time he was nineteen years old. He'd had his city during the time Young Jeezy had the streets on lock with the trap talk and cocaine was in—that had been over fifteen years ago and now, it was much harder to find coke in the area.

It was a new era, so niggas who were nobodies were stuck in the past, lost in time, and unable to keep up with the new trends of fashions, drugs, or cars. If you weren't driving a foreign whip, dripping in designer names from head to toe, you were considered basic, and you'd never make it out of the hood with a bad bitch. You'd be seen as a low-budget nigga with a woman who had a house full of Raman noodle-eating little bastards, all with different daddies, who never came around to help their kids.

Last but not least, if you were out there trying to distribute crack cocaine to the crack heads, you definitely had no real business about yourself. Nowadays, everyone from eighty to ten was involved with the designer drugs. The list was long and included drugs which were considered uppers or downers. There was actavis or mud, percs, xans, Molly, ice, roxys, oxys, heroin, fentanyl, K-2, legal, space, epidorsoda, duce, loud, and the list goes on and on. Anyway, I ain't about to keep puttin' y'all up on this shit. I'm not tryna fuck around and get indicted fuckin' with y'all. But, even with all those drugs in high demand, of all the drugs mentioned, if you didn't have a grip on the synthetics underworld, it was best for you to just fall back and get the fuck out the way.

Back then, Lil' Hook had a plug and Roe Black didn't, so they were a hot commodity in the area. However, this time around would be different for him and he couldn't wait. He had a valid resource that would take him to an upper echelon in the game. Not only was Maliss a plug, he was a socket. He was locked in deep with the synthetic world, or at least he was about to be. He had plans to fuck the world up when he went through with his demo. He had taken a liking to Roe Black though I don't see how. He would to take him to the top with them not knowing Roe Black had never touched ten bands before in his life, and the most bread he'd ever had was the bread he'd just brought home with him.

Now, Roe was ready to retry his Frank Lucas tactics again and become the biggest drug lord in Alabama, especially since deep down that's all his heart ever really desired. He had just had his first taste of double digits and he was eager to fuck with Maliss the long way because he knew he could direct him to the riches. Then, he would shit on his hood and anyone who had ever did him wrong.

Paper Boi Rari

CHAPTER 11

ROE BLACK

The next day he was in the bathroom with his phone. He pushed the numbers in to call Maliss to let him know he had made it to the free world.

"Tell it," Maliss answered.

"What's up, big bruh," Roe Black said, in an excited tone.

"Roe Black? You in that bitch, huh?"

"Yeah, homes, I'm out this bitch. It's on now. Shit, we just waitin' on bruh, but it's all comin' together. What the lick read though?"

"We in motion. I'm just gon' say that 'cause we don't talk on phones. The FEDs will take the simplest phrase and use it to describe a word; however, a word specialist will define that shit and make it a felony in court, my nigga. We got to get dem encrypted phones, then we'll be a lil' safer. We gon' link up in a sec," he said. "Keep yo' nose clean and get on up outta there. I should be on a leg monitor sometime next week, feel me?"

"Hell yeah, I'm on your heels like dead skin, bruh. Straight up."

Maliss started laughing. "Already. So, what's up wit' that SBA deal I asked you to check on?"

"Well, they got all kinds of workshops that train people on the best ways to obtain and pay off bank loans successfully. I understand they also give you the format on how to operate a business successfully too, bruh," he said. He looked out the stall to make sure none of the staff had crept up on him. "They help you write your business plan in whatever field you interested in," he said.

"Open up as many businesses as you can then stretch the ones that generate the most cash into every community. Franchise, franchise, franchise! Get your ideas ready," he said. "Give it your all so it'll be a successful vessel. Whatever you put your energy into should form and operate as close to perfect as possible, just as you seen it in your mind before it was built. It's a reflection of self, first. And second is cause and effect—in other words, your cause will affect us all," he said. "It's effect the ideals, your investments, and your money. And if that's the case, you gon' be um. . . let's see how I should put it," Maliss paused, "unfortunate," he finally said.

"You right, bruh. As of now I just wanna ponder on the things I can conquer and get paid for before I express 'em to you, homes," Roe said. He peaked out the stall and thought he'd heard the sound of keys jingling.

"Fa'sho, you do that. You know what the weak link to the chain now?" he asked. "It makes it difficult for the rest of the chain to perform at its best. Because the weak link is about to shut down and break, it can't keep up and needs to be removed in order for the rest of the team to move as one, Roe Black. This shit ain't for everybody. Niggas agree to shit for their own selfish reasons knowin' damn well they can't handle the position they accepted and agreed to," Maliss explained. "In the end, they deteriorate the whole structure of things. They end up regretting they were ever involved at all instead of keeping it G and acceptin' every angle that comes at 'em," he paused. "Nothin' is mastered on the first try. It takes practice and going through malfunctions. Basically, my nigga, experience brings the best wisdom in life, feel me?" Maliss asked.

"I'm on it, my nigga. Shit, I'm wit' it. I can accept it and handle it however it come, bruh," Roe said with enthusiasm.

"It's the only way. You gotta face that shit head-on. Shit, it's good you out, bruh. I'm glad you hit me up too. Gone get yo'self together and I'm 'bout to get up out this bathroom, boy. Fuck wit' me. One," he said.

"Bet that. You already know. One," Roe Black said, before the two ended the call. *I gots to fuck wit' homes, that nigga serious for real, boy,* he thought. He exited the stall and went to his room and unpacked his things.

It was Wednesday, April 17, 2020, his first day out of the FEDS.

Paper Boi Rari

CHAPTER 12

Maliss was on his way to work when he got the worst news he'd ever gotten in his life. When Drake's ringtone played through his iPhone, he knew it was his mom calling since that's the tone he'd programmed her call under.

"Mornin', Momma, how you doin' on this beautiful day, Sunshine?" he said, upon answering.

"You need to hurry up and get here, baby! I just pulled up to *The Spot* and, baby, it's in bad shape," she shouted through the receiver.

"Slow down, Mom Dukes, what you mean *it's in bad shape?* What's goin' on at *The Spot?*

"It's burnt down to the ground, Son! The fire marshals are here doing a special investigation to determine the cause of the fire. How far away are you?" she asked.

"I'm on my way. I'll be there in a minute," Maliss said.

"Wait, Son, before you hang up."

"Yeah, Ma, what is it?" he asked, hoping nothing else had happened. The news about his shop was all the bad news he could take in one day.

"You do have insurance on the building, right? 'Cause that would cover any damages to the building and replace most, if not all, your inventory. So, even though it's a loss right now, you really don't have much to worry about, except maybe having to find another location. Once you figure out how long it's gonna take to do that and restock, you can just let all your customers know. God got you, it's gonna be alright, Son," she told him. She was so sure he'd taken the necessary steps to protect his business, she'd went on and on before he could answer her question.

Shaking his head from side to side, he took a deep frustrated breath and replied, "No, Ma, I never got around to puttin' insurance on the place. To be honest, it slipped my mind once I went to prison unexpectedly. Oh my God!" he yelled out angrily. "Umph, umph, umph, umph," he said, as he weaved his way through traffic. I can't believe this right shit. Damn, Hawk gon be blowed behind this shit 'cause he the one who really love all this speaker stuff," he said.

"What the hell you mean *no?*" she yelled, matching his tone. "*It slipped yo' mind?* What the hell is wrong wit' y'all young folks?" She looked at the phone as though she could see his face. "That's the first fuckin' thing you shoulda did when you opened up the business, Maleek! Smart people protect their property, Son. I don't know where in the hell you got yo' business sense from. Well, damn! You got to be kiddin' me? A person proclaiming to be so damn smart!" she said in a raised tone. "Let me find out!" She shook her head. "I'm talkin' 'bout all the sense you claimed you had and turned out to be dumb as hell!" She laughed out loud at him. "Boy, I tell you, you never know until it presents itself, I guess. Niggas be puttin' on! They'll do everything under the sun to deceive somebody as if they got shit under control, just to gain control of the people they want to believe in them," she said. "Only to find out you were a fraud all along. The people who followed you were sad individuals too whose comprehension zero. They couldn't catch on to the shit you introduced 'em to, shit *they* believed they liked," she said.

"Ma!" he said, in an effort to get her to stop ranting.

"*Ma*, shit! Nah, they tryna keep you happy while you build your self-esteem and keep providin' delusions. In the end, all y'all turned out to be equally dumb," she said, shaking her head. "Smart enough to open a business, but slow as hell at the same time. Not remembering to protect your assets just earned you the World's Dumbest Business Owner Alive award!" she told him.

"Ma, okay, okay, okay! Stop, I get it," Maliss interjected when she paused momentarily. You can leave it alone now, please," he shouted, tired of her nagging and ridiculing his mistake. "I'm pullin' up now.

"I wish I would stop!" she continued. "I'm just gettin' on you wit' yo' slow ass. You must'a got that dumb shit from yo' daddy's side of the family, nigga," she said.

"Man, bye, Ma." He hung up as he skidded to a park. He jumped out of his car and made his way up to the building to witness the damage that had been done. The building was nothing more than a nice pile of ashes. Onlookers gawked at the scene in disbelief and fire marshals rushed around taking pictures and looking for clues as to what caused the fire.

Paper Boi Rari

CHAPTER 13

Ma Dukes continued to go in on Maliss because, in her mind, he was too smart not to cover his ass with insurance. Now, everything was gone, and in order to get it back, he would have to pay for it out the pocket.

If you recall being put up on game earlier, his business accounts were tied up in investments dealing with the black market, which included different types of synthetic street drugs, and Maliss had ordered a nice shipment of any and everything synthetic—from keys of heroin, Molly, ice, and fentanyl, to xanax, percs, oxys, and roxys by the hundreds of thousands. He had syrup by the hundreds of gallons, and space by the millions in all flavors of ten, fifteen, and twenty gram packs. Everything was dirt cheap, from pennies to a dollar Coming straight out of Japan, it more likely that it had really came China, thanks to his partner, Asian T. He had already sent the deposit fee they'd asked for, which was thirty-five percent down.

Asian T had been fifteen years into a life sentence in the FEDS, for running a sophisticated ecstasy pills and counterfeit money ring. The estimated run time had been eight years undetected, and everything was supposedly imported from Japan to the U.S. Once it reached the U.S soil, it was alleged that it was distributed throughout the whole country. The beauty salons, gas stations, cell phone repair shops, and nail salons were also alleged to be the home-bases for purchases. It was a billion-dollar tax-free industry. Of course, that's what the government hated more than anything. The government hated the fact that someone had the audacity to *try* and finesse their way through the U.S territory without cutting them in on it. On top of that, the Asians didn't share their money with the U.S. They would ship every dollar back to their own country, which only added fuel to the fire, considering the U.S. was in grave danger from debt to Japan. It was ludicrous for anyone to believe they could sell on the government's property, make enormous amounts of money for a significant amount of time, and think they would enjoy the money. It just wasn't gonna happen, not on their soil.

They were known to eat by extorting muthafuckas. If they couldn't get you for your money, best believe they would get you by giving you an ass-load of time. See, they knew giving niggas time would be harder on them because they'd never get that back since time went forward and never backwards. Add to that the restitution that had to be paid while you watched the time slip away from you—that's the government for you, they called it *justice*. You'll always heard 'em saying, "Justice for us all!" Check it though. It's *just us*, before *all of y'all* is what they really sayin' to us.

Asian T was a certified G though. He stood on what he believed in and fought for his innocence and was still fighting the FEDS today. He had that Midas touch in the streets, and his reach was both endless and limitless. He had that future shit going for him, you know, his name held weight. He also still had that bag so groovy, he had power. All his people were still in position out there and loved him unconditionally. They could make whatever he desired happen. He was definitely one of a kind. It was a privilege to even be in his company, an ever-bigger honor to be considered family to him. Asian T had freed his whole team and took the life sentence to protect the secrets from getting out, and to keep the FEDS from rebounding off of generations of hard work. Bet y'all can't say that bout nobody y'all know.

Maliss met Asian T threw making hooch, which was alcohol illegally made, and transforming it into moonshine. Asian T would buy every bottle Maliss could produce at a hundred dollars per bottle. Sometimes, Maliss would come down with ten to fifteen bottles at a time. Asian T would still want them all and refuse to let him go to the yard and sell any. He would cash them out right then and there or make one call. He was also known as Mr. Vegas since he ran a successful sport's ticket in prison and lived just like he should've been living, like a king. The two became super close. And when it was time for Maliss to go home, Asian T blessed him with a code to a site on the dark web, that would change his life forever.

Paper Boi Rari

CHAPTER 14

THE SPOT
Maliss and Mom

"Son, the fire marshals said the fire was set on purpose to cover up the burglary," she said, as he got out. "Whoever did it, broke in here and stole as much merchandise as they could and then set the place on fire.

"They wanted to make sure there wouldn't be any evidence left that could lead to them, huh?" he asked, nodding his head. "Not bad. It would'a been a pretty good tactic, and it probably would'a worked," he said, and paused, "if we were still living in the old days."

Ma Dukes looked around and then looked at him like he'd lost his mind. Then she stared at him and said, "Looks like it worked to me muthafucka! And let's not forget you don't have any insurance. Now see, them robbers was smart," she said, pointing at him then to the ashes.

"Alright Marshalls, thank you for your superb work in taming the fire, fellas. Good lookin' out, men, but seems your work here is complete. If so, you are no longer needed. Could you please leave us?" Maliss asked politely.

He emailed Hawk while he waited for the men to clear out. Once they were gone, he walked through the wet remains, kicking over different objects, here and there.

"Maleek, what are you doing? You are not a child anymore, playing in everything you come across. It's over! Gone!" She threw her hands in the air.

He started laughing at her. "I love you, Ma, and you too old to be cussin' like you some sailor, straight up."

"Who the hell you think you talkin' to though, Maleek? Huh? Tell you what, I ain't too old to get on yo' ass out here, nigga! Fuck you talkin' 'bout?" She balled up her fist and stood in a fighting stance. "Nigga, don't forget I'm straight up out that

Eastside of Detroit where niggas get killed just for walkin' cross a muthafuckas lawn."

"Come on, Moms, you know I know," he said. He reached down to pick up what he'd been looking for.

"What's that?" she asked, pointing to what he was holding.

"A fireproof camera with a built-in recorder. Thanks to today's advanced technology systems. See, least I had something for insurance," he said, smiling at her.

"So why didn't you let the authorities know so they could catch them fuck niggas? I told you, you so smart you dumb!"

"Nah, Ma Dukes, when they start that up? After I left?"

"Start what, Maleek?" she asked dumbfounded.

"Helpin' the police. What you talkin' about, Ma?"

"You stupid, boy. But, okay, yeah, you got me there."

"You know I'ma take care of it myself," he told her.

"Okay, Son, but be careful 'cause I need you more now than ever. Since I won't have no work to do in here for a while, I might as well head to the casino and play the nickel machines."

"You cheap, Ma!"

"It's called being conservative and reserved, Son."

"Cheap is what it's called," he said and laughed.

"Whatever, boy. I love you, Son." She kissed him on the cheek and turned to walk to her car.

"Love you too, Ma. I hope you win a lil' somethin'-somethin.' I'll talk you to later though. He stood and watched her leave before getting back to the business at hand. "Now look at this shit." He looked around the shop again and mumbled, "Niggas forcin' my hands to have to pull a demo. "Let me text Roe Black real fast," he said. He exited the perimeter of the burned down structure, hopped in his vehicle and skidded before hitting Roe up.

CHAPTER 15

MALISS and ROE BLACK
Proper Preparation

Maliss made it to the interstate in no time. Roe Black had sent him a text asking him to call him, so that's what he did. "You'll see my nigga. It's gone work, trust me. I've been in there twice, bruh. That's how I use to get my me-time in, homes," Maliss explained, as he talked on the phone to Roe.

"Bruh, that was how long ago? A year and some change? Shit, nigga, times done changed. What if the folks slide up there and check and I'm not there?" Roe Black asked.

"If they do, so what?" Maliss responded. He moved the phone away from his ear, looked at it, then mean mugged it as if he were looking through it at Roe. "What the fuck they gon' do, bruh? Long as you can pass the piss test you good, homes. You want this bread or what, nigga? I told you we on it. People believe in what they can see, and if they don't see us, they don't believe it's us, feel me?"

"Yeah, I hear you, but a nigga ain't tryna go back to jail, nigga," he said.

"My nigga, you worried 'bout the halfway house? You ain't said shit 'bout this bread or the details yet? Relax and listen to the rest of the plan so we *won't* get caught, nigga," he said. "'Cause right now, you throwin' me off wit' all that what if this, what-if-that shit. On Sunday I want— Nah fuck that, do it today for Monday, just in case yo' manager don't come in, or come in late," he said. "Put your move in on the kiosk for six hours to the Family Guidance Center, from eight a.m. to two p.m. They already know at the halfway house so it's gon' get accepted, bruh."

"A'ight, give me the run down on the demo," Roe Black said. Trying to sound game all of a sudden.

"I'll be there to pick you up at the gas station around the corner on Court St.," he said. "Then we gon' slide down to

Auburn real fast and take out a loan for four hundunn. It's thirty-eight minutes away from Murda Town. It shouldn't take us no more than two minutes tops, in and out. We gon' make it more like forty-five seconds though!"

"Yeah, yeah, keep goin', bruh," Roe said, as he hung on to Maliss' every word.

"So, all together, that right there makes what? Seventy-eight minutes, right? Maliss knew the answer but needed to know Roe Black was paying attention.

"Right," Roe agreed.

"Okay, it won't take me longer than ninety minutes to get down there and back," he said. "So that's right at two hundred fifty-eight minutes, which gives us a total of four hours eight-teen minutes, right?"

"Um, let me see, sixty times four is two forty. Bruh, it's correct, leavin' us wit' eighteen minutes to spare into the fifth hour. Continue."

Again, Maliss already knew he was right but needed to make sure Roe Black was still paying attention. Plus, he wanted to know if Roe would be reliable if he needed him to solve any problems. This would get his mind used to strategizing, so he would be capable of seeing his options fluently and naturally. "That leaves us an hour forty-two minutes to put yo' bread up and get back to the Family Guidance Center. I'll have everything we need to pull it off so don't trip," he said, as he waited for the light to turn green. "What I need to know now is where you gon' put yo' bread? I need to calculate it into the time, bruh."

"Shit, my BM stay off Fairview behind Churches Chicken. We can slide over there off the interstate and I can hide it in her backyard while her funky ass at work," Roe said, finishing his food from Flying Jay's Truck Stop.

"We good then. It's a go, that's another fifteen minutes to the Family Guidance Center. But we we'll be behind when we include the two hours it'll take for you to get back on the bus. What I'll do is drop you off at Krystal's, and you can walk back to the halfway house," Maliss concluded.

"Sound good to me!"

"Fa'sho. I'll be ridin' in a blue Mustang GT wit' eight hundred and forty horses, nigga. Straight for hot pursuits. It's a hot pursuit killa. This just a lil' start up to get yo' dick out the dirt." Maliss told him.

"Bet that up. This shit risky, ain't it?" Roe asked.

"Check it out, the greater the risk, the greater the rewards, homes, real cap. We straight, bruh, trust me. We in the same position in a halfway house, feel me?" he asked. "Always remember this, they can't stop what they can't see, and they will never know what they don't know. Them there partner are facts."

"I can dig it," Roe said and chuckled.

"I'ma see you on Monday morning then, bruh, one," Maliss said.

"Bet that up. One," Roe Black repeated and hung up.

For some reason, Maliss felt as if this were déjà vu. He lay down and thought about the dream he'd had in prison. He could see his shop as it was being broken into, all his shit and dope being stolen. Now, he was investing in dope, and out of the blue his shop gets broken into and burnt down. He hoped he was just tripping but for some strange reason it kept bothering him because in his dream the culprits had been some well-known car thieves from the city. He couldn't wait to check out the video and see what it would reveal. On top of the dream there was all the strange questions Roe Black had been asking. He understood the position they were in but that was all the more reason it was better to pull it off now. Who would ever think they had robbed a bank when they were supposedly working or looking for work? The fact that they were both in halfway houses for the FEDS was a plus so no one would suspect them.

When a muthafucka get to asking weird questions about shit they supposed to be a hundred percent down with, you better take head and reevaluate your plans and subtract them from it. Those are the signs of a rat that lets you know they not ready for the consequences the act at hand carries, my nigga.

Paper Boi Rari

I was trying to figure out what the hell was wrong with Maliss my gotdamn self. I wish I could have yelled and stopped him. I couldn't though, 'cause I'm only here to witness the story then describe it to y'all in full details and explain what really happened. Because we all know there are two sides to a story, and then there's the truth, or better yet, what really happened. For the ones who be like, man, this can't be true, I wonder what really happened? This is where I come in at. See, what really happened was . . .

This nigga askin' all these fuckin' questions and shit, fuck wrong with him? Nigga let's get this bread like we discussed. Nigga, I'm always against the police. Fuck the FEDS, Maliss lay there thinking about his dream and his current situation.

CHAPTER 16

MIKE Da BARBER
Outta Space Cutz

Later that evening the Flat Head Boyz pulled up on the southside trailing each other. The rides were beatin' like crazy as they swerved in and out of lanes until they parked in front Mike Da Barber's Barber shop: Outta Space Cutz.

Mike Da Barber was average height with an athletic built. He rocked a high maintenance dope-boy ball head and rocked a full beard on his face. He had moved to the 'A' from Florida to further his dream of wanting to become the best barber in the entertainment era. So far, he was *that* nigga to see in the city, and no one could slice like him.

He had hooked up some well-known artists and they had begun shouting him out in their lyrics. He had graced a few videos and was in the newest Lil Baby and Gucci Mane video. 1st Degree was known to be there on a regular, and Future, the Migos, and Ray J would fly in to sit in his chair. Yung Joc, T.I., Young Dro, and Drake were all in his *Cutz of Fame* collections. Lil Baby, Gucci Mane, Kevin Hart, he had all them boys under his clippers, and even O'Bama had been through there.

Mike Da Barber had come up off the cut game. It was a way of life of him. He put his heart and creativeness in his work. Being able to see a vision was a gift. He could create a trend in a moment's time with his clipper-game. He got paid handsomely for it and the game played fair with him. He had gotten a tattoo of himself as he lined up Rick Ross' beard, done on the back of his head. He'd gotten it done at Black Ink Atlanta. He had a pair barber scissors tatted between his thumb and index finger, on his right hand. He had the two-tone cream and cranberry Wraiths out front, sitting on 6s with the chrome Ruccis.

He attracted wealth to his shop. When the celebrities had started going, so did the high-end dope boys. His barbershop was no different from any other when it came to the gossip. Everybody talked about everything and everybody. Of course, like any other place, where there was prey there was bound to be Jack boys and prostitutes, and car thieves like the Flat Head Gang. He also ran a hood-rich gambling spot afterhours which consisted of craps and Georgia Skin, and he'd get all cuts from the pots.

No one would ever suspect him to be a vicious Jack boy. He had come straight out the trenches of South Florida, and he had been all over the world enhancing the murder rate for the love of money and the need for drug's. He was cold, and he moved by himself, period. Whenever he went to get it, he always came back with it.

Mike Da Barber lined up Fat Ant. Fat Ant was gwaped-the-fuck-up, to say the least. He was a heroin king out of Zone Six but ran Atlanta with that boy. He was a big arrogant nigga who thought he couldn't be touched so he put his business out there. We all know *anybody* can get it. At least, we *should* know.

"Yeah, Mike Da Barber these niggas be comin' short on a nigga check but beat me gettin' mad when I get mine out the product," Fat Ant said, looking in the mirror as he got his lineup done to perfection. "Got me fucked up, man. Shit, we gon' always be even, bruh. A nigga ain't owin' me shit out here. It's for keeps, homes, anything can happen. This the streets, feel me, bruh?"

"Hell yeah, bruh. 'Cause they ain't gonna wanna come clean if something was to happen. You catch hell tryna collect yo' bread," Mike Da Barber said. He stepped back to check if Fat Ant's line was straight.

"Okay. Already. Like Lil Dank. Check it. This nigga gettin' all this gwap out here, suckin' the streets dry for real out there in Douglasville. You know he eatin' wit' all them rich-ass crackers out there, right?"

"Yeah," Mike said. That was info that would be used instantly. He made a mental note of it since his brother stayed out that way, by I-20.

"So this stupid nigga get five of 'em but end up bein' short like thirty-three or some shit," he said. "You know me. I reached right in there and got me a lil' under a quack off of it. The nigga beat me gettin' mad, homes," he said.

"Nah, bruh," Mike said like as if he was really shocked by what he was hearing. He never talked much and everything he said was always kept short and complexed.

"Straight up, so I got all my shit and told the lame I'm good and was 'bout to clear it right? The stupid nigga came up with the rest right outta thin air.

"Nah!" True to self, Mike replied in his usual short, complexed manner.

"Yeah! A cold magic trick. Fuckin' fake-ass niggas can't keep it real to save they life. Why would you try to play the socket? I'm the reason the power transferin' to you. Without me, you ain't got no juice, feel me? I feel Boosie, bruh!!"

Mike Da Barber laughed. "That's real now. That's why I'm on the low, homes. Niggas catch amnesia quick," he said.

Fat Ant got up and checked himself out in the mirror, even though he didn't really need to. He gave Mike some dap and said, "A'ight, my nigga, good lookin' bruh. You keep a nigga in the fab."

"Man, you know I try my best, feel me?"

"You know you got the sauce, homes, no cap!" Fat Ant told him.

"Good look." Mike thanked him.

"Already. I'ma fuck wit' you, bruh. I'm 'bout to hit it, might stop by The Flame right fast and see what's shakin', you heard?"

"Straight up. Be safe, homes, I'll see you sooner than later, might stop by there myself," Mike Da Barber said, walking him to the door.

"One," Fat Ant said and made his exit. When he got outside the door, what he found was an empty parking space. His sixty-three AMG G-Wagon was missing—the Flat Head Gang had struck again.

Mike Da Barber was ready to go out and pay Lil Dank a visit one time. He figured he was worth, at least, one point five if he was coppin' five at a time, for a bill ten a piece with no pressure.

He was ready to suit up ASAP to get to them free bands, thanks to Fat Ant. *Fat mouth Ant, good lookin', my boy,* he thought, as he locked up the shop.

CHAPTER 17

AYESHA
A Scorned Baby Mama

That same night down in Montgomery, Alabama, Ayesha was also plotting up some shit on Maliss.

"You should get forty-five hundred back anytime within seventy-two hours to seven days. See, I added everything in you can get without gettin' audited," she said. She turned the lap top around so her customer could see the numbers for herself. "You see it?"

"Okay, Nicky. Girl, you already know I trust you so stop playin'. You been doing my taxes for the last three years without incident," Shawn said.

"A'ight, Shawn, drive safe on the road 'cause it's comin' down out there and the wind is blowin' hard too, girl. Call me if you have any questions though, girl."

"I got you, Nicky. Kiss Gabbie for me, and you need to let me come get her so she can play with London from time to time. And you know if I can't see how to drive I'ma pull over and put the hazards on until it calms down some out there, bae," Shawn said, standing up to leave.

"Better safe than sorry, and I'll keep that in mind. I be so busy, and Gabbie so stubborn and anti, I just let her be, child. But we'll see," Ayesha said, waving her hand in the air for added dramatics.

"Thank you, Nicky Baby." Shawn waved playfully and called Ayesha by her nickname.

"You know you good wit' me, boo, later!" Ayesha said, getting ready for her next customer. She was working late at her tax preparation business. It was April and she was going hard trying to get all her last-minute customers in before they charged points for being put in the system late. She would get hers free regardless, but the more she got in without incident, the more clientele she would likely gain the following year. She always gave two hundred percent when it came to her customers. She understood without them, she couldn't eat. So making sure they were satisfied was her only concern because that would almost guarantee her an excellent word-of-mouth reference. With that, she'd gain more customers to help put food on her table, and the help was welcomed since she was a single parent with two children.

She was a beast when it came to playin' with them numbers. She had mastered it, and everyone in the Tri Area was fucking with her—from Prattville, AL, Greenville, AL, and her home town and country, Lowndes County. She resided in Montgomery, AL. now, and they were even coming from Mt. Meigs, AL. She was definitely booked.

With all the competition out there, she worked hard to build her brand. She had outsmarted everyone with a sale's pitch she'd picked up from her baby's father, Maliss. *"Drop your prices down lower than anyone who threatens your sales. Watch how all the customers they thought were loyal check out on they ass. Once you get 'em, you cop, lock, and block 'em,"* she remembered him schooling her. Those were Pimp Rules 101. The customer received cheaper prices with greater quality, which meant faster results with the same, if not more, on their returns. Plus, her ultimate and unique sale's catch was doing under-the-table taxes after hours with a black-market site she'd found though they charged a higher percentage to put the taxes through. But it was worth it since her illegal taxes went through them. For every person her customers referred, they'd receive five hundred dollars and that—in and of itself—made her the tax queen of the south.

Ayesha was stacking bread so fast she had to invest in another building. She opened on the Northside and started directing customers in that direction, so her hands were full. Plus, she'd just opened up her own club which she named Club Impression's. The club was scheduled to have its grand opening tonight.

She knew she had to stay focused and on top of things so she eventually had to start moving her bread around to cover her tracks if she wanted to stay under the IRS's and FEDS's radar.

With the amounts of paper she'd been taking in she needed to do everything humanly possible to avoid wire fraud, identity theft, mail fraud, bank fraud, and embezzlement along with money laundry. Each crime fell under the illegal business she just happened to be into, and all had their own consecutive time ranges which would be collaged together in the end, *if* she were to ever get caught. That would also leave her stuck with an outstanding restitution to pay back, along with a lengthy amount of time to serve.

"Next," Ayesha called out. She was tired and ready to get finished so she could leave.

"Hey, girl. How you doin' up in here?" Joanna asked.

"I'm good, girl. I gotta hurry up though. I mean, I might able to take care of three more of y'all after her but it's a wrap until tomorrow after that, y'all," she told them all. "I'm sorry for any inconvenience this may have caused. Please drive safe out there in that weather. And if y'all can, come by Club Impression's tonight. Y'all know it's the grand opening and I got Future performing, plus that nigga J Deezy the one opening up for him with his hot single: Favorite Room the Kitchen. They out in this weather for me, and a check always come first," she said, excitedly.

"I'ma be there," someone said through the sea of customers.

"A'ight," another said.

"You know I'm gon' be there," another said.

"Future?" The female's excitement was all Ayesha needed to hear which confirmed her attendance.

The loud sound of the doorbell rang as the customers filed out one by one, just like Ayesha had filed their taxes. They had money on the way, and now they were en route to get ready to show up, show out, and par-tay.

"So what's up, Joanna? Let's get this shit poppin' 'cause I can't be late for my own celebration, feel me?" Ayesha said, She snapped her fingers in true-diva fashion. "Shit, that would be like bein' late to my own funeral, girl," she said. They both giggled.

"Well, I'm tryna clear about eighty-five hundred this year."

"Let me see, you got three infants, right? They gon' bring you twenty-five hundred a piece so you lookin' good already, bae, A'ight let me see," she said. She typed the keys on the keyboard quickly. "Um, okay, there you go. I got you right at eighty-eight hundred, Joanna. You should receive your return within seventy-two hours to seven days." She turned the screen toward Joanna and pointed out the return date information to her.

"Thank you, girl, you are the best!"

"Don't trip. This for us. If they got it to give a way, you know I'ma get it for us to enjoy, bae. You drive safe and make sure to stop by my club."

"I'm not gon' make it tonight, maybe another time. I gotta go get Samuel's dinner ready for work, girl. Congrats though, sweetie, and enjoy yourself."

"Will do," Ayesha said. "Next!"

CHAPTER 18

After Ayesha finished with her customers, she went in the back, took a shower, and got sexy from head to floor.

"My ole' bitch-ass baby daddy wanna fuck wit' a bitch, and start shit? That muthfucka know I ain't on all that 'cause I finish shit," she said aloud, as she walked around office. "Nigga, we *forever* no matter what." Right in the middle of her rant, she grabbed her stomach. "Damn, my stomach hurt." She barely made it to the bathroom before she threw up everywhere. She stood and made sure she was done and rinsed her mouth out. Then she headed to the front of the office, turned off all the lights, and locked everything up.

After hopping in her ride, she hit the Blvd, headed to her club. "Maleek, you gon' wish you never shitted on me," she said, as she stopped at the red light. "Once I finish wit' you, you gon' have to move out the country, nigga. 'Cause yo' bitch-ass must'a forgot I got yo' social security number and birth certificate." Ayesha was so angry she continued to converse as if he were right there in front of her. The light turned green and she pulled off, still babbling. "Yeah, nigga I'ma be watchin' everything you do. And just like the song say, 'I'm gon' tax that ass'." She laughed. "I'ma hurt that ass the way you 'sposed to hurt a real boss nigga. And you know how I'ma do it, baby daddy? I'ma hurt them muthafuckin' pockets, nigga," she said, and pounded the steering wheel.

She pulled into the Club's parking lot. "So, go ahead, 'cause I already know you 'bout to go off out here and run it up. And when you do, I'm gon' be right in the cut, ready to jump off the muthafuckin' Trump Tower and bring yo' shit crumblin' down." She laughed out loud, looking at how packed the parking lot was. "I'ma suck all that bread right out yo' accounts and into my offshore accounts, and yo' dumb ass won't be able to do shit about it 'cause you won't be able to trace it." She laughed again. "Umph, I know how to finesse 'em too, nigga, and I'm 'bout to show yo' ass." She turned the car off, checked herself in the mirror, and kissed at her reflection. "Gotcha!" She winked at herself, put the visor up and got out of the car.

Future's voice could be heard in the parking lot, booming through the speakers:

> Woo, everything we do, we goin' dummy (Woo)
> Whatever I do, I hope I got that Tommy (Hrrr)
> Just in case a nigga try to play, play, play (Just in case)
> Yeah, every watch I own on tsunami (Brrr)

When Ayesha walked in everybody was going dummy, reciting Future's lyrics word for word. The club was jammed packed wall to wall. There were bottles sparkling everywhere. Niggas was blowing bread, and since tax refunds had started dropping the bitches were splurging too. She knew she had killed them with this one. She was the ex of a hustler, and she had soaked up the game and utilized it on whole 'nother level. She was about to do everything she could to capitalize off what she'd gained from Maleek. Then she'd turn around and use it against him.

"What you said, Maleek? First you get yo' bread which is the power, right? Then you go to war," she said. "Fuck-nigga you gon' wish you never met Ayesha," she said. She was mad and hurt because he hadn't fucked with her since he'd been released. Now, she was about to take great measures to hurt him back. *How you gon' stop what you can't see? You can't! You can't prepare for somethin' when you don't know it's comin', or who it is that's plottin' on you.* Umph, umph, umph. That might've been the most vicious and reliable insight you *ever hipped me to, Maleek,* she thought to herself, as she made it to the office inside the club. She laid her phone down. "Now, let's see how smart you are, will you be able to reverse this shit?" she asked out loud to no one.

She sat down behind the desk in the club's office. She stared at Future through the mirror-tinted window, as he performed hit after hit, looking just like her baby's daddy.

110

Kingpin Dreams 2

"I seduce you with this Aston Martin I bought today / oh you then did more drugs than me? You must be hallucinatin'/ oh you did more Perk's then me? / you must be hallucinatin' Future rapped. As he worked the stage.

"Oh, you think it's over, baby daddy?" she mumbled. Then she began to freestyle her own bars:

> "You must be hallucinatin' / oh you thank you the only
> one who can finesse/ you must be hallucinatin'
> I just killed 'em for some free bands
> you couldn't get me down if you gave me zans
> oh you got mo' game then me, baby daddy?
> you must be hallucinatin,'"

She put the money through the money machine and sipped on Ace of Spades Champagne from a flute. She took small sips and made sure not to drink too much because she wanted to keep her mind clear to plot and plan against Maliss. Ayesha was the epitome of a scorned baby's mama.

Paper Boi Rari

CHAPTER 19

MALISS and ROE BLACK

Monday, April 29, 2020. 8:03 a.m., Maliss sat at the gas station behind the wheel of the GT, smoking on a Kool 100, as he waited for Roe Black to get there.

The vineyard was already getting heavy traffic. It was a known drug spot and they had it all over there—it was a real one-stop shop. The city bus rounded the corner coming off of Fleming Rd., onto Court Street.

"'Bout time! Damn, it's 8:05. Black folks always late," he shouted, in an agitated tone.

The bus came to a stop and opened the door. Roe Black stepped off in a hurry and got in the car. "What it do, bruh?" Roe Black asked, as he closed the door.

"What's up wit' it," Maliss replied. He dapped him up and pulled off into traffic. It was perfect-lick weather because it looked as if it was about to storm, meaning the police would be very still, plus they couldn't drive but so fast in the rain. The day was exactly the way Maliss liked it to be when carrying out a crime.

"Boy, boy, I say, boy, you couldn't have picked a better time, my nigga. I know they ain't comin' up here now, not in this weather, 'cause it's 'bout to pour down out this bitch," Roe said, peering out of the passenger's window.

"Come on, homes. Stop playin'… this what I do my nigga. I play to win! Rain, fire, and time are three elements to beat any crime, my nigga, 'member that! What really tops the day of is the date, my nigga. It's the 29th," Maliss told him.

"What that mean?" Roe looked over at Maliss with his forehead creased up.

"It means the bank gon' be full, my nigga. I couldn't say all that on the phone. I knew 'bout the rain and all, but once they burned my shop down, I had to put somethin' in motion ASAP!"

"Hell yeah, bruh, you sho' right. They 'bout to cash them checks on the first and third, ain't they? Oow-wee, boy, boy, boy. I say, boy, they gon' be loaded, ain't they? Right on time! Boy, I say boy, you a genius." Again, Roe looked at Maliss, this time in amazement at how smart he was.

"Cut that phone off and take the battery out too. I'm tellin' you now, they can trace all kinds of shit like that."

"A'ight, I'ma turn it off now," Roe said. But, instead of doing as he'd been told, he only pretended to turn it off, and put the phone on silent instead. He kept talkin' as he did it to throw Maliss off. "Let me see my mask and shit." He opened the bag and saw some gloves, a black long-sleeve shirt, black no-name running shoes, black Levi jeans, black knock off Ray Ban shades, a black T-shirt, and a black GLOCK 40. "A'ight, all this is good, but where the fuck the mask at, bruh?" Roe rummaged through the items in the bag still looking for the mask.

"Nigga, the long black sleeve ninja mask. You remember how to do it, don't you?" Maliss asked, looking over at him.

"Oh, hell yeah, that's cool. That throwback shit, huh?"

"That shit gone scare the shit out them folks, huh?" Maliss asked and laughed.

"Straight up." Roe Black pulled the sun visor down and tried it on.

***

Thirty-eight minutes later, they were in Auburn off of Toomer Street and West Magnolia Avenue, in front of an Auburn Bank branch. There were three cars already parked there. Maliss had already Googled it, so he knew that the white and red car belonged to the employees and the truck belonged to a customer. He drove to the next street, where he and Roe changed into their gear. Once they were suited up, he drove back over to the bank. The white truck was still there. He pulled in the parking lot and right up to the door. Leaving the car running, the two jumped out but left the doors cracked.

When they entered the bank, they noticed a black man at the counter depositing his check, and a black teller waited on him. The teller looked to be around five feet six, about one hundred seventy pounds, and cute with shoulder length hair. Maliss guessed her age was in the early thirties.

Standing right next to her was an older Caucasian lady who looked to be in her mid-fifties, tall and thin. She had her attention focused downward and appeared to be texting on her phone. She never even realized the danger that was lurking. A much older lady sat with her back turned, facing the drive-thru window.

By the time the black female teller finally noticed what was about to take place, it was too late. She saw two masked men coming toward the counter at full speed. She screamed and fell to the floor, covering her ears. The Caucasian lady remained calm as if she were taking in all details. The customer squatted down and put his hands up high in the air. The older lady still hadn't realized the robbery was taking place. She looked around eighty-three years of age and Maliss figured her hearing aid was probably turned down. By the time she did look in his and Roe's direction, they had already jumped over the counter. By now, the time was 8:43 a.m.

"Everybody get the fuck down now and don't look at us! Get down! Get down! Get the fuck down now! Don't look at us! Maliss yelled, shouting out instructions. He had on a Rasta hat with the bib pulled down over his mask, and that was the only difference between he and Roe Black's gear.

"Don't move and step back!" Roe Black said. He ran up on the white lady and held his pistol on her. "Now . . .," he spoke calmly, "we need one person to tell us where the fuckin' vault at!"

The black teller on the floor yelled out, "It's back there." She pointed to a small back room.

"Is it unlocked," he asked.

"Y-yes it-it's unlocked."

Roe went to check it. While he checked on that, Maliss cleared out the first teller's draw. "It's locked," he yelled over to Maliss. Next, he walked back over to the Caucasian lady and grabbed her by the neck. "Go open that muthafucka up," he said through clenched teeth, as he pushed her toward the vault.

While the vault was being opened, Maliss was still putting money inside a white pillowcase. He looked at the door and noticed a man coming toward it. The man looked as if he'd seen a ghost when he finally realized he was looking at masked man. Maliss stared at the man and shook his head *no*, instructing the man not to enter the building. Of course, the man took heed and scurried off. Maliss couldn't say anything about the potential customer who had just tried to enter because he didn't want to scare Roe Black. And by the time he cleared the drawer the vault was open.

"Come on, come on, Come on!" Roe Black hurried the woman along, coaching her to move faster.

Maliss ran over with an opened pillowcase. The thin white lady stepped back but didn't take her eyes off them. She wanted to give the best description she could to the police.

"Hurry up, hurry up! Come on, come on, come on!" Maliss said. Coaching and motivating him at the same time.

"Let's go! Let's go!" Roe Black called out to Maliss, pulling on his sleeve. He was ready to go but Maliss was trying to get more cash.

"Got it!" Maliss said right before they beelined it out of there.

The time was now 8:44 a.m. It seemed like it had taken forever to the people on the floor when in reality, the whole robbery had taken 60 seconds. In one mere minute, they had cleaned the bank out completely. And just like that, they were gone with four hundred sixty-three thousand dollars.

The thin white teller ran and locked all the doors and attempted to get the tag, make, and model of the car. Maliss was too smart though, he had removed the tag ahead of time. She ran to the phone and called the police while the older lady sounded the alarm.

Maliss hit the gas and the GT did not disappoint one bit. They disappeared with the quickness. He pulled over and put the tag back on and then took back off.

"Hell yeah, boy, did you see all them hundreds?" Roe Black asked in a hyped tone.

"Nah," Maliss said. He was calm since he was used to getting money, and even he did see them, so what?

"Let me show you real fast!" Roe said a child opening a present on Christmas.

"Man, hell nah, nigga! Where the fuck my cigarettes at?" He hit eighty-five south headed back to Murda Town.

"Man, we straight! I see what them niggas talkin' 'bout now! This shit is sweet! Yes, sir," he said, animatedly. He was beyond excited and the feeling was euphoric. Maliss knew he hadn't seen any real bread right but he didn't trip. He figured he had to start somewhere. He smiled and put on *Pure Cocaine* by Lil Baby:

When you rich like this don't check the forecast/ everyday it's gone rain/ made brick do a flip can't whip up/ this pure cocaine/ from da streets but I got a lil sense/ but I had da go coup no brain/ I aint worry 'bout you, I'mma do what I do and I do my Thang! Boom! Boom! Boom!!

He turned it up as they rode down the highway, thirty thousand shy of a half million. They vibed all the way back until they reached Roe Black's baby mama's house and parked in the back. They divided the bread up and ended up with a total of two hundred thirty-one thousand five hundred a piece. Roe Black grabbed ten bands and hid the rest in the backyard. They left there and headed back so Maliss could drop him back off at Krystal's.

"A'ight, bruh, be safe and be sure to spend light, my nigga. This shit gon' be all over the news up to a fifty-mile radius, so chill and don't go crazy just 'cause you got it, nigga. You should still be straight off the prison demo for real."

"I got you, bruh. I'm good, but shit they ain't gon' think it was me anyway. I'm in the halfway house, homes. How the hell I'ma rob some shit?" Roe Black asked and laughed at loud at his own humor.

"Just listen to me and trust me, my nigga. I know what the fuck I'm talkin' 'bout. Fuck where you at. If you fuck up, they gon' find a way to make it stick," Maliss said, "and get rid of that phone, nigga." He pointed to it.

"A'ight, a'ight! Bet that," Roe said. They dapped each other up and Maliss vamped, leaving him at Krystal's to walk back to the halfway house.

Maliss might as well have been talking to a wall because Roe went and did the exact opposite of everything he'd told him to do. See, little did he know, Roe had made plans of his own in case something went wrong.

Fuck the FEDs, Roe thought, and stared spending money like it was going out of style.

CHAPTER 20

AGENT SMOOTE

At approximately 10:10 a.m., April 29, 2020, Agent Smoote had the thin white lady from the bank sign her statement. Her name was Tina Rich and she was the bank's manger.

"So, this is your statement which you find to be true and correct and give at your free will, to the best of knowledge?" Agent Smoote asked, as he looked at her.

"Yes, I do." Tina answered. "If I think of anything else I'll give you a call, sir," she said, looking her statement over, before handing it over to him.

The statement read as follows:

I, Tina Rich arrived at Auburn Bank at approx. 7:30 a.m. on Monday 29, 2020. I arrived a little late on due to waiting for Dollar General to open and it opened at 7:00 a.m. Upon arrival at the branch, I put my drinks in the fridge for the day, clocked in, and signed into my sessions before getting my teller drawer out for the day. I noticed the blinds in the office were pulled open which was the non-verbal sign for all clear. So, I let the blinds down and began assisting customers for the day.

I waited on approximately (approx.) ten to twelve customers. During this time, I noticed the clock since I'd always check the mailboxes across the street. At that time it was approx. 8:30 a.m. eastern standard time. Since I knew Ginny would be taking lunch at 11:00 a.m., I knew I had a few minutes.

So, at approx. 8:45 a.m., I was in the process of looking down at my phone checking an incoming text message, when I heard the front door open and put my phone down. When I looked up, I was met by two black males, one held a black gun. Seconds later, I was now looking down the barrel of the gun. He demanded I put my hands up at that time, so I did. The two men jumped over the counter.

One of the gunmen waved the gun around while yelling at Candice, Ginny, and Will who happened to be the only customer in the building, not to try anything funny. Ginny was at the drive-thru, Candice was on the floor in front of the small vault, and Will was in the front lobby with his hands up. At that time, I made eye contact with the gunman, but he quickly stated not to look at him.

The other gunman asked where the money was after taking all the cash from Candice's drawer. Candice told him it was in the vault. At the time he wasn't able to get in due to the gate being closed. The one who asked walked me to the vault to unlock it with the gun pointed in my back. At the time I was in the big vault, I could hear the gunman outside the vault rushing the other one along as he continued stashing the cash inside of a huge pillowcase.

At that time, I noticed the shoes of the men which were a no-name-brand type of black tennis shoes with black shoestrings. One of the men had on white socks and the other had dusty ankles and no socks. One had on a black shirt, black gloves, black jeans, and what appeared to be, some black-colored nylon wrapped around his face. He had on a yellow braided hat. The other man wore the exact same thing minus the yellow braided hat.

After they took all the money they jumped back over the counter, ran toward the door, and exited the building the same way they came in. One carried the gun and loaded money bag, and the other, a gun and a cellphone.

The one thing that stuck out most was, I noticed as the guys were leaving, the first one had to be familiar with our branch because he didn't use the right door, he used the left one, and our right one remains locked at all times for safety measures. Only someone who visited the bank often would know that.

I got a pen and piece of paper to take the tag number down, only there was no tag. It was a late model Ford Mustang with white lettering that spelled out the word Mustang. They sped off going towards the interstate. Ginny hit the alarm while I called the police. By that time, the time the Game Warden had arrived at the location, and now, the Federal Marshals.

Signed: Tina Rich 04-29-2020

Agent Smoote read over the statement. "Thank you, Ms. Rich. If you have anything else please contact me," he said, handing her one of his cards.

"Will do. Thank you," she said. She headed back inside the bank to lock it up for the rest of the week.

Later that day, Agent Smoote was back at the federal building watching the video footage. He had started his investigation and had already hit the hood, but he still hadn't come up with any leads—there were no snitches and no suspects yet.

Paper Boi Rari

CHAPTER 21

MIKE DA BARBER
In Black Sometimes

Mike Da Barber sat outside a three-story house in Douglasville, GA. He was dressed in all black including a Drako and a nail gun. He was waiting on Lil Dank to come home so he could get paid in full. He had found out everything he needed to know about Lil Dank. Now it was show time. It was 1:58 a.m., and he knew Lil Dank would be in no later than 2:45 a.m.

"He should be here any minute," he said aloud, as he waited. Like clockwork, Lil Dank pulled in, piloting a black SL 600. As the garage door went up, he drove in and pushed the button for it to close after he'd gotten inside. Right before it closed all the way down, Mike Da Barber slipped inside, gun drawn, book bag on his shoulder.

Lil Dank got out and went to the trunk and pulled out duffle bag filled with money. Next, he headed toward the door. His old lady opened the door for him wearing a lingerie set, ready to get her fuck on.

"Hey, baby. I hope you ready 'cause I been waiting all day to ride that dick," she said, with her hands stretched out, so that they touched the door frame on both sides.

"I'm good and ready, bae," he replied.

"Me too!" Mike Da Barber said.

BAP! BAP! He hit him upside his head twice with the pistol.

"Argh!" He screamed out, still clutching the bag.

"*Argh*, hell! Get yo' bitch ass in the house, nigga," Mike ordered him, catching him and his lady by surprise.

"Noo, please don't hurt us! We will give you whatever you want, just don't hurt us," Ni Ni said, with her ass jiggling all over the place. She was super model, fine to say the least.

"Everybody shut the fuck up, and you get yo' ass in the fuckin' house like I said, nigga," Mike Da Barber said. Holding the gun in one hand, and the nail gun in the other, as soon as they entered the house, Lil Dank made a move and tried to break for it. He tried to pull his gun out and take cover but the structure and set-up of his home was too open. He was determined not to give up anything, plus it was a man's nature to protect his domain. Only this time, protecting his domain proved to be a deadly mistake, and the worst move he could have made at that critical moment.

SWOOSH! SWOOSH! Mike Da Barber let the nail gun sing the whisper chorus for him. It hit Dank three times out of five shots, two in the back, and one in the leg which caused him to fall on contact. One of the shots went all the way through the wall. The nail gun was powerful enough to shoot seventeen feet away. The other one went straight into the three-year-old little boy's eye as he was running to his parents to see what all the noise was.

"Aghh! Aghh! Umm, no, no, man, not my little boy! Lord, please! Get up, Darall! Get up, Son, daddy's here. Come on, Darall, get up and come to daddy," Lil Dank pleaded as his heart broke in two. Lil Dank was hurt badly but he was still crawling to his son's aid. It was useless though because Lil Darall had died instantly without even knowing what happened. He never even had a chance to make a sound from the powerful impact. Mike Da Barber had loaded three-inch nails in the nail gun, and the nail had gone all the way through Lil Darall's eye socket and into his brain. It had stopped moving when it reached the back of his soft skull, which allowed the tip of the nail to stick out a few centimeters. His little body lay on its back in a puddle of blood with his eyes open, blood oozing out.

"Nooo! Stupid muthafucka, what the fuck have you done, huh? No! Please, baby, get up, it's gonna be alright! It's gon'—"

SWOOSH! SWOOSH!

Ni Ni was cut short when three shots came from the Drako with the silencer on it. Mike Da Barber put three in her head silencing her forever while reuniting her with her son. She fell back like she was playing a game of limbo. Sitting on her knees, her back and head touched the floor from the powerful impact of the Drako. Mike showed no remorse for them. He was there for one purpose, and one purpose only: leave everything dead, and leave with the money and drugs.

(M. O. A.) Money over all and (M. O. E.) Money or else were the rules he lived by.

"Fuck! Fuck! Fuck! Man, damn! Nigga, you didn't have to kill 'em! You didn't have to do that, man. I woulda gave you what you wanted, man, damn!"

"Nigga, you still gon' give me what I want," Mike Da Barber said.

"Umpf!" He kicked him in the side, rolling him over onto his back to face him.

"Arghh," he screamed out.

"Now, what's it's gon' be? You join them, or you give it up and live to try and create another family? The choice is yours, homes. I already got this bag right here so fuck it," he said. "But this just this one means death for you, so I need every thang and then I'ma be on my way, Lil Dank."

"Umm, ahh, ahh," he moaned in agony, "it's upstairs in the master bedroom at the foot of the bed. Ahh," he moaned "pull the door up." He coughed. "Twenty-two, seven, nineteen. It's all there. Everything, man, I swear!"

"We'll see. Turn yo' ass over. Don't want you to go nowhere while I'm gone!" He put the zip ties on him and connected him to his dead girl so he would definitely be there when he returned— unless he could pull dead weight.

Lil Dank gave him what he wanted since his twin girls were still sound asleep. He knew he had to try and have their lives spared especially since he was partially to blame for half of his family being killed just moments prior. The twins were all he had left.

Mike Da Barber went up stair and cleared the floor safe. He came up on nine and a half kilos of raw heroin, and three point two million in cold cash. He checked the rest of the house before going back downstairs and that's when he came upon the two little girls sound asleep in their bedroom. They looked to be about seven or eight years old, he guessed. He closed the door back and spared their lives for the system to distribute the struggle to them. He knew they would be mentally fucked up anyway, once they realized their mother and little brother was no longer with them.

"A'ight, you lucky it was all there like you said, homes. Good lookin'. For that, I'ma spare yo' life *this* time. See you around, my boy," Mike Da Barber said. He picked up the first bag from the floor, threw it over his shoulder, and headed toward the door. Just before he exited, he turned around, stood with his son and baby's mama, and into afterlife.

He eased out as smoothly as he'd entered in and vanished into the peace of the night. Mike had left a horrific murder scene, a scene unusual for that neck of the suburbs.

After leaving the area, he went the fuck off and reached his highest pinnacle in life. He'd become a multimillionaire overnight.

CHAPTER 22

TALLADEGA, AL.
FCI Free at Last

7:25 a.m., July 5, 2020. Maliss sat in Talladega, AL. FCI parking lot waiting on his brother-from-a-different-mother and Ms. Andrews. They hadn't spoken since their last conversation. *She should be pulling up any minute now* he thought. He was moving back up once again. He had his trap in Sin City doing light numbers just to look like he was trying. It was just a front since he was the one doing most of the trappin' for that specific area.

He sat behind the wheel of a brand new 2020 Benz truck. It was glacier-blue on chrome Rucci 26s, with seashell-colored interior. The truck had been a gift from him to Hawk. He was killing the drug underworld and selling the synthetics hand-over-fist. The streets gravitated to them like chameleons. Enough wasn't enough for him though, and he was addicted to the free bands. It's all profit and never give it back. Now that Hawk was out, he could put his real plan in motion.

Maliss had also brought Lehya and Sonya along as a welcome home gift for Hawk. Hidden behind the metallic tint on the windows, the two women sat in the back seat playing with one another, geeked off the synthetic Molly.

"Damn, 'bout time," he said, looking at his Richard Mille—it read 7:48 a.m. He'd made sure to park in the space beside the one Ms. Andrews parked in.

A few minutes later, Ms. Andrews pulled in and parked. She was turning her phone off and checking the Benz truck out. She was trying to be nosy and see inside but it was impossible. "Somebody ridin' in style," she said out loud. She grabbed her handcuffs belt and got out keeping her gaze locked on the truck. Her uniform was skin tight and it showed off her curves in 3D. Even Lehya and Sonya found themselves checking her out.

Maliss slid the window down about an inch or two. "How you get into them pants Miss? You think they could get any tighter? Who you tryna pull? An inmate?" he asked, as he peaked out the window.

"Excuse me?" she said. She stopped abruptly and put her hands on her hips. Turning toward the truck, she rolled her neck the way women do when you piss them off. Squinting her eyes, she strained to see who she was talking to.

"I said how did you manage to get them pants to accommodate them curves like that? 'Cause I don't see no slack in 'em at all!"

"Like any other person get their damn clothes on. Furthermore, I don't talk to stranger's and I ain't pressed for compliment so keepin' your thoughts to yourself would be the best option for you. You need to just wait on your people to get out!" She turned around and didn't wait for a response before heading for the entrance. She switched harder-than-a-muthafucker and her ass was eatin' them pants up.

"I ain't know I was a stranger though," he called behind her.

He stepped out of the truck wearing Versace slides with the black and gold Medusa head on them. Black Versace shorts were paired with a black and yellow Versace silk short-sleeve shirt that also had the big face Medusa head on it. With that, yellow Versace suspenders with the black Versace symbols decorating the front were attached with the Medusa head gold clamps. On his eyes were a pair of clear lens Cartier, with the gold symbols embodied in cherry wood on the sides. 14K gold Medusa head earrings blinged out his lobes, and the eyes, which were made from red rubies, set them off. The yellow Versace ankle socks brandished the name brand symbol all over them. The fragrance of Bond No. 9 graced his skin and had him smelling rich as fuck. He pointed to himself, pinky ring glimmering hard from the VVS Medusa head. He had one on each of his pinky fingers, set in a gold base with the ruby eyes. To top it off, he had seven small 14K gold ropes with the VVS Medusa heads also with ruby-red eyes, and there was small charms on all of them. He was fuckin' the streets up. Real cap! With a black and yellow Bust Down Richie Millie, and the black Versace belt with the Medusa gold head with the red ruby eyes belt buckle, he was drippin' a little over half a ticket on his flesh, without even trying. The true definition of a walkin' lick. His wicks were hanging long, and he was shining like new money.

None of it meant shit to him, and he always remained humble at the top just as he was at the bottom. He just liked to dress in his best, and he believed a person should always go out looking as good as possible. In his opinion, a person's presentation was worth trillions alone. A man's first impression was the permanent impression people would expect of them. Now your bed is where you will spend a third or more of your life. So you should want the best material to lay on for the proper and appropriate sleep available. Sleep like a king! Right now, he looked like he'd just robbed one of them mummies in the pyramids in Egypt.

When he stepped out of the truck, Ms. Andrews was completely caught off guard. She regrouped and smiled at the sight of him. "Yes, you are a stranger. You don't think so?" she asked, half smiling and half mean mugging him.

"That's news to me, to be honest," he replied.

"And why is that?" she questioned. "You don't reach out to me. I see you got yo' weight up so that's probably why you don't have time to answer your phone or text and shit, huh?"

"Nah, it's never that," he said.

"What is it then? What? You get off on seein' how long I'll keep tryin'? I mean, what the fuck, Maleek? I'm not no stalker or no shit like that. But I been tryna reach your nappy headed ass for two months nigga and you ain't said shit back," she said. "Communication is the only way we can build. If that's not gonna happen we can't bond in no other kinda way. I ain't with the mental games you seem to be gettin' a kick out of playin'," she said, pointing at him. "You good though, I see life treatin' you fair. Since you here I'm about to find out right now though. Where we go from here?" She put her hands on her hips and waited for his response.

"Well, you know I gotta keep it real with you."

"I hope so. It's the only way in my book." She stared at him.

"A'ight, most people hate the truth and rather be lied to, or rather you would have lied to them once honesty finally reveals itself," he began.

"I understand, but I want the truth any day of the week. That way I always know what I'm dealin' with. Plus, that lets me know what my next move needs to be." Ms. Andrews was serious, and she wanted the answers she'd been trying to get since he's been released.

"VerAysha, I think you sexy as hell, no lie, bae. I also understand you need stability in your life, right?" Maliss asked.

"Right, so what's the problem? I'm just dying to know, Maleek. So, please hurry up 'cause I'm 'bout to be late tryna figure this shit out."

"I do want you in my life, VerAysha. I wanna show you a journey of adventure and excitement and much more. But being the type of dude I am, my life is complicated. To deal with me you gotta be out-goin'. You feel me?" he asked. "In order to have me you have to be able to share. You feel me? You can't be a selfish person and you can't be jealous hearted either. You have to understand and trust me with your well-being and know I'ma always be here for your every need and want. Trust that I know how to manage and handle your insecurities without doubts, VerAyesha," he said.

"You seem like you touched on all basics of what I'm lookin' for. The sharing shit caught me off guard though, and *jealously*? What you plan on doin' to stir up them kinds of emotions in me? I ain't wit' the sleepin' wit' any female you want shit now!" She rolled her eyes.

"Me either. Basically, I'm sayin' in these days and times I can't function with just one female, love. I have to have a variety of them to keep me experimentin' and enjoyin' life. No disrespect to you as a woman. I need all my woman wit' me under one roof, VerAyesha. I'ma provide for all of them and give them all the appropriate attention needed, feel me?" he said. "You only live once. Me personally, I refuse to live a borin' normal life while I'm here. It gets borin' with one woman moanin'. As couples, we get tired of bein' around each other after time passes, and the sex will become average. The female starts to complain about bein' satisfied and she blames the male for it when it's really both of them. As humans we become slaves of pattern," he said, looking at her as he paused for a second. "To avoid this, I need a loyal fleet of smart woman who want the same thing as me outta life. We all stick together and do our parts to make sure we get what we want and need in life," he said. "So, now, since I finally explained this to you, this is why I been avoidin' you. I wasn't sure you would understand my way of life. I respect you enough not to hurt you or mislead you. Now I put it all out there for you, VerAyesha. I would love to have you on my team so we can share a different experience in life. So, what do you say?" he asked.

She looked at him as if he'd suddenly grown three heads on his shoulders. "Maleek, who the fuck you think you are? Don Juan or Pimpin' Ken, one of them nigga's or somethin'?"

"Hell nah, 'cause I ain't tryna make my woman fuck for money to take care of me or no shit like that!"

"So you think you can maintain a fleet of women all at once with no problems? With all the emotions we deal with and the different personalities we have on a daily?" she asked.

"I know I can because we gonna get an understandin' of how this whole ordeal will function. Everything has a format. You can either fuck it up or you can get the best performance out of it. So what's up? You fuckin' wit' me or nah? Try me out one time. You can leave whenever you like if you ain't happy. I'm sure once you get a taste you won't be able to live a normal life again," he said.

"Yeah, Maleek, I'll be a girlfriend of yours. I'm tellin' you now though, I require and demand a very lot of attention and I expect to get it when I want it," she said. She was kind of shocked from his boldness, but it had turned her on at the same time. She had never even thought about being with another woman. But, the way he'd put it, had her curiosity getting the best of her. She also wanted to see another way of life aside from the one the normal routine she'd seen all her life.

"That's a fact! Now come here and let me feel on you," he said, holding his arms out, for her to fall into.

"Nah, I'm 'bout to go to work. I got one minute to be on the clock," she said. She stepped back from his reach.

"Man, you with me now, bae. That job shit over with. I got you from now on. Now come here like I told you. I been waitin' to squeeze on all that ass you got back there too? Stop playing now," he said, stepping in closer.

Ms. Andrews strutted over and fell into his arms and inhaled his elegant aroma. He kissed the corner of her lips and gripped her ass firmly before smacking it hard for the cameras. Lehya and Sonya looked on with lust in their eyes. Neither could hardly wait for the orgy to start because she was definitely a bad bitch.

"Come on and let me introduce you to our two girlfriends before my brother get out here," Maliss ordered her.

"You got two girls already? I wasn't the first one? We 'bout to have problems already, nigga," VerAyesha said.

He started laughing. "You trippin'! I had to present this to you how it came, baby. Everything happens when it's time for it to happen," he said smoothly.

"Yeah, a'ight," Ms. Andrews said, following his steps.

He tapped the window and it slid down a third of the way. Lehya and Sonya smiled, showing off two pair of beautiful perky titties. "VerAyesha, this Lehya right here," he pointed. "And this is Sonya," he said. "These my sexy, bad-ass, fine Asian girlfriends. Lehya and Sonya say hi to our new old lady and make her feel welcome into our family," he said.

"Hey, VerAyesha," they said at the same time.

"What's up, y'all?" VerAyesha said, admiring their beauty.

"A'ight. Y'all all gon' kick it in a minute," he informed the three women. "Let the window up. Y'all showin' off all my shit," he said, with a playfully.

"Okay, daddy." They giggled coyly.

"I don't share my women either, but I made a one-time exception for my brother, Hawk. I'ma let them fuck him back to society on our way back to the A."

132

"I ain't doin' no shit like that," VerAyesha said, frowning up her face.

"You gon' do whatever I ask you to do to make me satisfied, VerAyesha. Don't tell me what you will and won't do again because I finalize all the decisions being decided and made. Not none of y'all! I wouldn't ask you to do nothin' on that level unless it was necessary for us to gain profit as a whole, understand?" he said. He looked at her with a stern expression.

"Yes, Maleek, I understand," she said.

The door came open and out walked Hawk, dapping harder than Jerome Rome off the Martin Lawrence show.

"Free at last, free at last! No papers, no halfway or nothing," he said, as he made his way over to Maliss.

"What's up, my boy!" Maliss said, smiling hard.

"Shit, a check, nigga! You already know!"

"I'm tellin' you," Maliss replied. They embraced a brotherly hug and gave one another some dap. Hawk checked him out head to floor, shaking his head in approval of what he was seeing. He already knew Maliss, so he knew from the looks of things it was back on.

Hawk was draped in an all Prada short set, burgundy top and bottoms with black Christian Louboutin loafers on.

"Let me introduce you to my three girlfriends, my nigga." Maliss smiled big.

"Three girlfriends?" Hawk was impressed.

"Yeah, you already know Ms. Andrews, right?" He pointed.

"Yeah." Hawk nodded his head.

"A'ight, well her name is VerAysha. Me and her just became lovers while I was waitin' on you. Now come here real quick." He went to the window and once again it came down before he could tap on it. Lehya had Sonya's titty in her mouth while fingering her. Hawk smiled because he knew Maliss was a wild nigga. "This is Sonya here, bruh." He pointed again. "And that there is Lehya. They my personal property, but until we make it to the city, they

gon' bless you down on the strength of me. So go crazy, my boy!"
He dapped him up.

"Bet that up, big bruh! I'ma handle that fa'sho," Hawk told
him. He was smiling at them and they were smiling at him. He
pulled out a pack of Prada condoms. He was about to open the
back door and thought about what kind of whip it was. "I thought
you said, you was comin' in a rose truck, nigga?"

"Nah, what I said was, you was gon' make enough to afford
one by time you got out. Fuck you talkin' 'bout? Won't get me
like that!" He started laughing.

"Oh yeah, that's right, that's right," Hawk said, shaking his
head. He got in the back with the girls and got naked right away.
He put his dick in Lehya's tight, warm awaiting mouth and she
sucked greedily.

Sonya ate Lehya causing her to give an even better head
performance on Hawk. Next, she got down and rode his tongue,
blocking out the sounds he wanted to escape from his mouth.
Lehya's tongue and jaw game caressed his dick so tight, he knew
he would explode at any moment. She had the neck gift on lock.
He was getting served right in the parking lot.

"VerAysha, I'm following you to your spot so you can drop
your car off. Then, we can get you to your new residence. Don't
worry about packing anything, I got you," Maliss said.

"Okay, baby," VerAysha said, nodding her head, as she got in
her car, and pulled off leading the way.

CHAPTER 23

"Umm, ahh, hell yeah, right there, right there." Hawk was enjoying himself in the back seat. Lehya was slow-neckin' the head of his tool in and out with vacuum-tight suction. Sonya licked and sucked his nut sack. "Damn. Oh, yeah, just like that," he moaned.

Lehya was geeked up and she was rotating her head and neck as she went all the way down and back up on Hawk with a nut-busting rhythm. She had zoned out on his dick. He had leaned up on one elbow and started rubbing and pulling her toward him, feeding her the dick. Sonya decided to give her a break though she didn't need it, Sonya just wanted in on the action. Lehya went and got her kitty tightened up while on break.

"Ah, um," Hawk sounded out. Sonya was swallowing his seeds down without leaving a drop. She continued to suck him and made sure to keep him hard for the rest of the treatment they had in store for him. Finally, she climbed up on his dick and slowly grinded her pussy while pressing her hands down hard on his chest.

"Oh, um, Sss, I'm cummin," she screamed. She began to shake violently.

Hawk grabbed her by the hips and picked her up and down on his massive dick, slamming her down so hard, edge of his nuts seemed to go in and out of her pussy, right along with the dick. When he felt himself on the verge of climax, he started ramming it inside her.

"Ah, ahh, yes, yes, yes!" Sonya reached another epic explosion. She eased off resumed sucking him as a display of her sexual gratitude.

VerAysha had made it home and made it in the truck just in time to catch Lehya's backwards-cowgirl performance.

Lehya grabbed Hawk's shin, leaned over, and started bouncing her ass down hard. She made it clap in his face while milking him with the vice grip her pussy had on him.

"Lawd hah mercy, girl! Damn," Hawk said, as he rubbed and smacked her ass hard. When he stuck his finger in her anally, she screamed out.

"Ow, ooh, ahh." Lehya and Sonya both were pure freaks and they'd been fucked in every hole imaginable. They loved being pleased and enjoyed pleasing others even more—man or woman, old or young, they didn't discriminate. And the fact they only dealt with ballers or men whose pockets were deep, was an added bonus.

Hawk released his grip from her waist and bent her over in the doggy-style position. He grabbed the top of the back seat and kneeled behind her. Then, he grabbed her hips with a firm grip and pushed himself as deeply inside her as he could go and humped once with force. He began to fuck Lehya so hard she attempted to climb the seat. "Un-uh, where you goin'? Huh?" He slammed into her. "Huh?" He pounded again and again, digging her back out real good.

"Ahh, oww!" She came again and quickly moved out of his path.

Hawk grabbed Sonya instead and directed her to lie on her back. When she did, he pushed her legs behind her head and held them there as he frog-fucked her. A thick white orgasm shot out from her hole but he kept pounding.

With a final grunt, he pushed himself in her one last time and allowed his first nut in the free world, to explode like a firecracker on the 4th of July.

VerAysha was so turned on by the action, she leaned over and started giving Maliss some of head. Taking him by total surprise, it caused him to swerve before quickly regaining control. His toes came off the gas but he put it on cruise control.

By the time they passed the Six Flags Amusement Park, everyone was satisfied and worn out.

Hawk was back out and shit was about to go from zero to a hundred, real quick!

Paper Boi Rari

CHAPTER 24

AYESHA
Fraud Queen

Life was treating Ayesha like the Queen she was, and she was receiving blessings on top of blessings. She really had no stress at all in her visual, except one thing, and that was: no matter how much success she gained, nothing could keep her perplexed like Maleek Davis aka Maliss. No matter what, she could not get the stain he'd left off her brain. She hated him with all her heart. In less than six months of being released, he was already ahead of the curve. All her friends kept up with his Facebook posts and IG pictures. He was the topic of conversation every time they hooked up—Maleek this, Maleek that, and she would be able to share no info because he barely even corresponded with her. When he did, it would always be dry and short.

> Ayesah: Maleek? When r u going to come get Gabbie? U do have a daughter who needs her father u know or do u?

She pressed send on her phone, sending out the text message. A text came right back from Maliss.

> Maleek: Yeah. I know I got a daughter and I'll be down there in the next couple of weeks if it's God's will. Right now my schedule is tight for real. I can't wait to see her. I miss my princess!

She opened the text and read it. Then she sent another one.
> Ayesha: Well why u don't face time her so she can see ur ugly face sometimes? BITCH :(

She texted him back.
He sent another text right back. She opened it up.

Maleek: FUCK YOU! STUPID BITCH! Stop txtin me lame ass hoe I'm busy! I'll be there when I get there. I dnt need u to remind me CUM SUCKER!!!

This made her furious with him. She turned on the news while she sat at her desk, in the plush office inside her club. She started punching in keys, searching for everything Maleek Davis had ownership of. She had one thing in mind, to take it all from him.

First, she Googled his name to see what would pop up on him. Part owner of The *Spot* which was an auto sound and speaker shop. Owner of a clothing line called *Start My Own*. Owner of *Bigger is Better*, a rim shop. Owner of *Seduction*, an exotic dancer's club. Owner of Place *Yo' Bets*," a sport's bar. Owner of an *Pent House,* and he also owned three homes in the upper scales of an Atlanta, GA. neighborhood. He had two homes in the upper scales of Montgomery, AL., and a house in Phenix City, AL. Maleek Davis was also currently pending a deal on a house whole name, *Illegal Activity*. It targeted a safe sex atmosphere with a line of different ideas, a modern trend to change the way the world sees sex. She finished reading and she was impressed, and even madder than before.

"Oh, bitch, you 'bout to be fucked real good," she said. aloud, as she read a little more. She couldn't believe how fast he'd gone up the chain of success. The way he was attacking the community was incredibly witty. She had to admit, she was hating really hard. She hit a few more keys and the news caught her attention. She turned the TV off mute.

Breaking news:
"Hi, this is Robin Medows and we have just been informed of an arrest on a Jamal Millz out of Houston, Texas, in connection of a missing four-year-old Meya Dickerson. Jamal Millz was the last person reported to see her. As he claimed, she was in her car seat while he changed the tire on his car. A neighbor turned over camera footage with Jamal leaving the scene with a clothes basket with what appeared to be a trash bag, wrapped around a small object with a few clothes in it. Meya Dickerson's

mother is now also claiming the child was abused and molested. It is confirmed that the blood found inside Jamal Millz' apartment matches the DNA belonging to Meya Dickerson. Jamal Millz is being charged with Capital Murder which he is being held for pending further investigation. This is all being that is being revealed as of now, please, stay tuned for more on this case. It's said he is being held at Houston County Jail. Stay tuned for a later update. This is Robin Meadows reporting live," the news reporter said.

Ayesha hit mute. "Umph, umph, umph! That's why I ain't trustin' nobody 'round my kids. These crazy ass niggas out here with they nasty asses. Fuck wrong with that bitch ass nigga? Messin' with that poor little girl. God, please put your shield around her and protect her soul Father God. Amen," she said, praying aloud.

She put Maliss' SSN, his birth date, last place of residence, his last car model, and then his mother's maiden name, and just like that, she had hacked into his bank account to do whatever she wanted to do. He was linked to four credit unions and two big banks. She went ham with his shit. She changed his address to one she had asset to, then ordered hundreds of thousands of dollars of shit in his name. After she did that, she cancelled all his credit cards.

"Press send if you would like to make a one-time transaction, press one to confirm and hear your new balance, Thank you," the automated operator said.

She cleared all his accounts out and transferred them to her off shore accounts which couldn't be traced or tracked. Once she finished, she placed a virus in his system. Every time he put his name, SSN number, birth date, or tried to deposit or open an account, it would automatically go in his account, at the same time, alert her and in seventy-two hours. It would automatically go into her offshore account.

After she finished, she couldn't but laugh at her own self. "Teach you 'bout fuckin' with me, baby daddy. Just a lil' child support for ya bae. I'ma tax that ass every chance I get, nigga," she said. "You 'bout to be mad as fuck, nigga. I'd give anything, except yo' money back,t to witness the look on yo' face when you find out. All I do, all I do, all I do is win, win no matter what," she said, mimicking the song lyrics.

She got up to pour herself a glass of Ace to celebrate her victory. She had just hit Maliss hard within minutes of what it had taken him to put in motion, but mere months to store up. Ayesha had just cleared him of forty-six million eight hundred thousand dollars in liquidated cash and credit. The majority of it had come from his business credit. He'd only had a million four hundred in cash that he could pull, but his credit was A1 off the finesse of the game he knew. It was just the same as liquidated because it did whatever he wanted and needed it to do. It only had a four percent interest rate. Ayesha had just smoked him.

"Shoulda had LifeLock fraud protection, baby daddy," she said aloud. She took another sip of her Ace and sat it down. She was killing herself laughing. She didn't want to drink for real though, because she'd just had a miscarriage a few months prior she hadn't revealed. The doctor said it had come from too much alcohol. Her fraud game was like that though, she could never lose that. She was the fraud Queen!

CHAPTER 25

TRAP STILL JUMPIN
J-Racks

J-Racks was moving product like it was '04 and '08 again when Meech was out there doing numbers. Only this time, it was the synthetics that was killing them. You would have thought he was swiping from the numbers he was seeing. Once again. he had the tri-area on lock, and it wasn't shit anybody could do about it. Except, of course, Maliss or the FEDS.

He had heard Maliss had opened a trap, on the southside by the LP projects, that was doing a little something. Nothing major, but since he had the city, that's all that mattered to him.

Today, J-Racks had brought out his 488 Spider Ferrari, triple blue. He was riding dolo. He was on his way down the road to the race and bet a few hundred thousand, just to kill time. This was an every weekend thing for him. The race was being held on a back road since it was illegal street racing. Street rules, street niggas, with real street bread. No polices interrupting you with all the bullshit, just straight dirty south, country niggas hanging out enjoying themselves. Niggas would be selling everything under the sun while they were betting on the cars they loved. Would be around eight races held on Saturday, and eight on Sunday.

> I told you muthafucka I be right back/ Shootin' dice in my hood must of lost eight stacks/ but I'm only ridin' this cause the Chevy in the shop/

Young Jeezy's ringtone came through his phone. "What it do, my boy?" J-Racks answered.

"Shit, I'm comin' through Union Springs now, fam," Slick Nick said.

"A'ight, once you get to the interstate, take it until you get to twenty-six, then come down there until you reach the first gas station, bruh. I'll meet you there. We should get there 'round the same time," Racks told him.

"Bet that. I'm on the interstate now, fam, and wait til you see these pits I got, my nigga. They all for sell except one, I gotta keep her. She cocoa-brown with a white patch over her right eye."

"Oh, yeah? What kind, bruh?" J-Racks asked.

"Razor edge and Gotti! Straight gamed. Super big heads bread for mouth and mass, my boy. They already trying to hit, fam."

"How old?" Racks asked him.

"Four months."

"Papers?" he probed further.

"Every single one," Slick answered.

"How many?"

"Four boys, three girls, excluding mine," Slick reminded him.

"How much?"

"We'll chop it up when I get there, fam. One," Slick said. and hung up.

J-Racks got the dial tone. "This young nigga wild." He smiled, looking at the phone before putting it on the charger. He was on Hwy 31 pushing the Rari hard with the top down.

Twenty- five minutes later they met up at the One Stop gas station down the road.

"Hell yeah, my boy, them bitches prettier than a muthfucka," Racks said when he lay eyes on the dogs.

"I told you, fam." Slick bragged like a proud father.

"I know I want two of 'em right now! I can gone tell you that, let me see," —he looked at the puppies— "I want this one right here and this one right here, my boy. What the ticket is?" He held them by their necks. He had picked an all-white boy with a black patch on his chest, and a girl that jet black with blue eyes.

"I can't accept no less than eight-fifty for the male and the female, for you? Just give me seven even for her, fam. That's love right there," Slick said. "But when we get to where we goin' the males are fiftteen, and twelve for the females, feel me?"

144

"Come on, lil' homie, say no more. Ain't no pressure, I 'preciate that, good lookin'. Here you go," he said. J-Racks handed it him fifteen fifty.

"Bet that up," said Slick.

"Fa'sho, let's ride then." J-Racks headed to his car.

"That's that 488, ain't it?" He was checking the whip out.

"This old thang? Yeah, that's it. You like it?" He asked Slick.

"You already know. That bitch is to die for, fam!"

"Nah, it ain't that serious, ni." Racks laughed.

"Shitin' me, it ain't!" Slick was in love with the ride. He could see himself cruising in it.

"Cut the shit."

"My nigga, in the city, they gettin' you outta there for one of my male puppies, bruh."

"Stop playin'!" Racks laughed louder.

"Since when have you ever known me to do that?" Slick asked seriously.

"Never." Racks' smile turned into a crooked grin. Slick was always so animated, and he found it amusing.

"A'ight then, my nigga, real cap!"

"Man, that ain't even a deposit on a lawyer, boy. They can only make what? Six commissaries wit' that?"

"They don't give no fucks, they want the name. Fuck the zoom-zooms and wham-whams," he said.

J-Racks started laughing. "You off the chain, my boy, follow me. They racin' up the street, and you passed right by it, actually," he said, pointing in the direction of the race.

"The hell I did. I ain't see nothin' in these woods but the trees wavin'."

"I know, that's the best part," J-Racks said, as they hopped in their rides and pulled off, one behind the other.

When they got there, the drivers were down to the last three races. Slick Nick ended up selling all his pups except his girl. Someone had offered him twenty-five hundred but he turned it down. J-Racks tried to jump on the offer but dude didn't want his.

Overall, they'd had a good time down there. Racks and Slick won a few extras, and everything was going good until the shooting broke out.

Cars were pulling out left and right. People were screaming and scrambling. All hell had broken loose about a race that had been set up. The shoot-out left two dead and no one knew anything. That's how it went down that road. Any time a crime happened it was always unsolved.

CHAPTER 26

MALISS and VERAYSHA
Some Me-Time

After Maliss had given Hawk the Benz truck and got him settled in, he sent Lehya and Sonya to Universal Spies to pick up some trackers and a few more listening devices. He had set up a nice intimate weekend for he and VerAysha. He wanted them to get some me-time in to help her adjust to the lifestyle.

He had covered a lot of ground since he'd been out. He'd been so busy he hadn't made time to relax and focus on his piece of mind. He cleared it with his P.O. so he was good to go. He was glad Hawk had finally made it home since it would take some of the pressure off of him for a while. His hands were full and there was still so much to be done.

As soon as he'd gotten his money right, he'd paid for a private jet for the whole year. The jet was a Hawker 400 XP. It cost him eighteen thousand eight hundred forty-five dollars up front, and three thousand five hundred ninety-five dollars per month, after that. He had also made reservations for Khao Lak, a private island, which was one of the quieter coastal destinations in the country. The island was in Thailand, two hours driving North of Phuket, a hot spot for celebrities, like Leonardo DiCaprio.

Maliss was going all out to surprise VerAysha and she was clueless to his plans. She had never flown in her life, and she was under the impression that they were going to the airport to pick up his niece.

He pulled up in front of the medium sized jet and got out. He walked around to her door and opened it for her.

"Come on, bae, get out," he said, holding his hand out for her to take.

"For what? I'm good right here. She 'bout to get off the plane anyway, right?" VerAysha asked unknowingly.

"Nah, she too young for them to let her off alone. I gotta board the plane and sign for her to get off. Once they verify I'm her uncle, they'll release her to me, bae. Now come on. I want you to see how fly the cabin is anyway," he urged her.

"Maleek, I ain't wit' all this plane stuff now. I'ma pass on it, for real," she said. "I'm good, I'll see it another time," she told him. "What's the name of it? I can just Google the name of the plane and see if they got any pictures of the inside."

"Woman, if you don't get out this car and come on, I know somethin'." He grabbed her hand and waited for her to get out.

"Man, damn," she said, pouting. She sucked her teeth. Realizing he wasn't going to let up, she stepped out in her Jimmy Choo sandals and white sundress. The dress was filled to capacity and it seemed to stretch with every step she took to keep her ass inside of it.

Once they made it to the jet, he helped her up the steps.

"Welcome aboard, Mr. Davis and Ms. Andrews. I'm Melondy, and I'll be your flight attendant for the remainder of the flight. Please, be seated and make yourselves comfortable as we prepare for takeoff. If there is anything I can accommodate you with, please, don't hesitate to ask. I'm at your full service. Thank you, and enjoy your flight," Melondy said.

How she know my name? I know I didn't just hear her say 'prepare for takeoff,' did I? VerAysha thought to herself. "Ahh . . . nice to meet you too, honey, but that won't be necessary. We're only here to pick up someone. Wait, Maleek did she say prepare for takeoff, bae?" She looked at him. He squeezed her hand and he knew she was 'bout to clear it. She looked at him through squinted eyes and tried to loosen his hold on her hand. She was prepared to make a run for it to get off the jet, but it was too late. The door closed and it was sealed vacuum tight as the jet allied up.

"Maleek, what the fuck are you doin'? You know I hate planes! Why you playin' right now, bae? Let me the fuck off this bitch right now," she screamed. She had turned straight hood, punching the side of the cabin with every word. Maliss remained calm. He smiled as he watched her carry on her tantrum. The plane

148

had begun to descend down the runway slowly, preparing for takeoff.

"You gonna love me when we get where we goin', bae. The only way to conquer fear is to face it head-on. Look, I'm even here to help you face it. Now, I just need you to have a seat and buckle up before the stewardess comes over here. Besides, once we get in the air, you might just end up on top of the ceiling showing off all your goodies. bae." He laughed and patted the seat beside him, gesturing her to sit.

"Fuck you, Maleek! I wanna get off this fuckin' plane! Now, damnit!!"

"Sit down and buckle up. Now," he said, letting her know he was serious. The jet taxied down, turned, and stopped as the jets opened up hard. She felt the power and looked around the elegant cabin. She noticed the flight attendant was also strapped in so she hurried and did the same thing. Just as she clicked her seat belt on, the jet picked up its speed and raced down the runway at two hundred miles per hour. And within seconds, it was off the ground and into the air.

"Ahh, God help me! Maleek, I'ma kill you as soon as I make it off this damn plane," she said. She closed her eyes tight.

The bell rang and a male's voice came through the speakers, "Please, make sure all electronics are turned off until we are leveled off. Today, is sunny with clear skies, wind at 7 degrees NW and 3 degrees SE. The time is now 11:25 a.m. ET. We are scheduled to land at 6:37 p.m. ET. This is a seven hour twelve minute flight. There will be no stops from Atlanta, GA. to Thailand, Khao Lak. Melondy is the flight attendant, and she will be here to accommodate and serve you on the way. Thank you for flying, enjoy the flight. This is Pilot Jessie James," the pilot announced, before getting off the intercom.

By now, VerAysha had started to calm down. She looked around and took in the décor and space of the cabin. It was astonishingly glamorous and fully loaded with Oakwood through and through. It was fully equipped with Oakwood desks, Oakwood tables, and Oakwood countertops. A forty-two-inch plasma hung in the front view and there was a fully stocked mini bar with an array of vintage wines and Champagne. The seats were plush, covered in seashell-white leather made from crocodile and trimmed in gold. There was also had an extended bedroom furnished with a king size bed and a sixty-five-inch TV on the wall.

"This is nice, Maleek, but I'm still gon' fuck you up when my feet hit soil, baby. Thailand, Maleek? Really? I don't even have a change of underwear," VerAysha said. She folded her arms across her chest and resumed pouting.

"You don't need any but we'll shop and make sure you get everything you need when we land. Right now, just relax and enjoy the clouds, bae," he said and paused. "VerAysha?"

"What?" she answered, glaring at him angrily.

"Welcome to the mile-high club, bae!" Maliss winked at her.

"Real cute, Maleek," she replied. "Real cute!" She cut her eyes at him.

May I be of any assistance to any of you?" Melondy walked up to their seat and asked. She licked her lips, staring directly at Maliss. Her mouth watered as if she could eat him alive.

"Well, yes. I'm quite famished to be honest," Maliss said, rubbing his hands together.

"Famished, Maleek? What, you went to private school too, huh? You just full of surprises today," VerAysha said. She laughed and shook her head.

"What? That's just proper English, bae, that's all. Nothin' surprisin' 'bout it."

"If you say so," she answered.

"Yes, Melondy. I would like the croquettes with wild rice, with butter-drenched steamed string beans and buttermilk crostini with a hint of Smucker's grape jelly please," he said, giving his order, "oh, and if you don't mind, can I get a glass of your finest white wine to top it off, please. Once I'm finished with that, I'd like a slice of peach cobbler for dessert. I'll also have some spicy mozzarella cheese sticks for the appetizer. Thank you, Melondy," Maliss said.

"Mmm, that's a wonderful choice, Mr. Davis. You *are* famished, huh?" the attendant smiled flirtatiously.

"Um, yes he is, ain't he?" VerAysha said, looking at him."

"And for you, Ms. Andrews? Would you like something as well?"

"Yes. I would like the grilled boneless fish dipped in wild mustard sauce, wild Spanish rice, hush puppies, tater wedges, and coleslaw. I'll also have a glass of white wine, please. For dessert, I'll have a slice of German chocolate cake with flaming marshmallows on top and a blow of French vanilla ice cream, please. The appetizer shall be pepper jack jalapeño cheese bites. Thank you."

"Excellent choice, Ms. Andrews! I'll be back in a jiffy with your orders," Melondy said.

"Looks like I'm not the only one famished here," Maliss said and chuckled.

"No, sir you're not. I admire your choice in food. I guess you're tired of pancakes, oatmeal, and cold cuts, huh?" VerAysha said. She couldn't help but laugh at her humor.

"Got jokes, huh? Didn't think I knew how to get my grub on or somethin'?" he asked.

"Nah, actually, I never thought about it until now. You got great taste all around I see," VerAysha said.

"Yeah, bae, only the best and nothin' less," Maliss told her.

After they got their bellies full, they got tipsy, flirted and fondled one another. They continued to kick it and play with one another for the reminder of the flight, until it was time to exit the jet.

"The time is 6:23 p.m. ET. The weather forecast is sunny with clear skies with winds 2 degrees SW and 4 degrees NE. We will be landing in approximately fourteen minutes. Please remain seated and buckle up for turbulence. I hope you all have enjoyed your flight. Please, turn off all electronics until landing. Thank you all for flying," the pilot Jessie James said.

VerAysha looked out the window. She was instantly blown away by the breathtaking view as they crossed the waters. It was crystal clear and you could see the mammals swimming. Some people were parasailing, some were jet skiing, and others played various water games. She saw a few surfers trying to catch a wave. The water was so clear you could see the reef from up there. She saw all the evergreen trees, and big birds she had never seen before sailing through the sky.

"It's beautiful here, bae! You got me way cross country in another world. Yesterday I could've never imagined anything like this," she said.

"I'm already hip, that's why I planned it like this. I knew you wouldn't be down if I asked you straight up so I had to finesse you just to get you to experience a different view on life. Plus, I needed a getaway to spend some me-time with you. And, at the same time, I needed time to get my thoughts together on the moves I'ma make in the near future."

"Prepare for landing in two minutes," Pilot Jessie James said.

"A'ight, bae, here we go. The second part to the flight, the landing. After that, you will have completed the whole cession," Maliss informed her Veraysha.

"I got that queasy feeling right now, bae. Other than that, I'm good. I'm ready to touch ground so I can beat that ass like I promised," she said, gazing at him.

He laughed when she closed her eyes. She prayed silently for their safety as they continued to descend to earth.

Once the jet landed, she was more than ready to do some shopping and sightseeing. She was looking forward to finding a few sexy bathing suits before exploring the island.

"Thank you for choosing the Hawker 400 XP Private Jet Club. Again, we hope you enjoyed your flight and we were pleased to be of service to you. Feel free to call on us anytime as we depend on you, to depend on us. We count on you to trust in us to get you wherever you need to be, at any time. Thank you, and enjoy your stay," the pilot Jessie James said, as they stepped off the jet.

***

The weather was beautiful. Maliss touched VerAysha's lower back, guiling her toward an awaiting Maybach S600. The chauffeur was an Asian belle. She was five three in four-inch heels. Her Auburn colored hair hung straight down the center of her back. Her weight was a hundred forty pounds which was considered thick for a woman of four eleven. Her measurements were 34C-25-41. Yes, Lord! Eye candy with an ass too phat!

"Hi, I'm Gina. Welcome to Khao Lak, Thailand! I'll be your chauffeur and guide while you are here. Don't hesitate to ask for anything you want. If it in my means, I will make sure you receive it. So, how was your trip?" the chauffeur asked.

"Very relaxing," Maliss answered.

"Where to from here?" Gina asked. She proceeded to hold the door open for them.

"Well, first, we need to go shopping for a few hygiene products and clothes. Could you take us to a few of the best high-end stores me and my lady will be pleased to shop in?"

"Yes, of course. I know the stores here like the back of my hand. Please, get in and get comfortable, and I'll take you to the exact spot I think you'd want to be, Mr. Davis."

"Thank you, Gina," he said. They got in and she closed the door.

"*Hi, I'm Gina,* Blah Blah Blah! Was she flirtin'? 'Cause I will beat her lil' Asian ass over here. Ain't no more Asians comin' in so don't try me over here, nigga!" VerAysha said, mockingly. "Fuck around and make Asian sauce out of her ass."

"I didn't say anything, you did," Maliss said.

"Yeah, a'ight. Play with it if you want to." She looked at him and her face displayed a serious expression.

As Gina whipped through the city, VerAysha was overwhelmed by all the mountains and bright colors throughout the city. She saw dragons on the sidewalks, dancing and beating drums, and people doing tricks with fire.

Gina continued to give them a quick tour of the city until she came to a stop in front of a Gucci store. She had no idea it was like dropping kids off in a candy store, especially since Maliss had enough to buy the entire store if he wanted to.

"Does this appease your taste, sir, or do I need to go elsewhere?" the chauffeur asked, after sliding the partition down.

"No, Gina, this is perfectly fine with us. We shouldn't be long at all," he said.

"Okay, sir. Let me get that for you," she said. Gina got out to get the door for them. "Take all the time you and the lady need, sir."

"Oh, we will," VerAysha said excitedly.

Maliss grabbed her hand and put his free arm around her waist and led her inside.

"Good evening and welcome to Gucci of Thailand. Have a drink please," the sale's personnel offered.

"No thanks," Maliss said, as he looked around to determine which way they would go first.

"Do either of you need any help?" she asked politely.

"Nah, we good. 'Preciate it though. If we do, I'll be sure to ask." Maliss smiled.

"Okay, sir. I'll be right over here." The nice lady walked off but made sure to stay within their sight. She could spot a big spender each time one entered the store, and she knew the commission she'd make would be big.

Maliss and VerAysha scoured the aisles of the store, sparing no expense. This was the first time VerAysha had ever been able to shop name brands on such a level, and she definitely wasn't playing. The two spent over an hour getting everything from underwear to summer wear, straight off the mannequin. Once they had gotten all they wanted, together, their total had come up to forty-two thousand seven hundred sixty-one dollars. Of course, that was pennies to Maliss. He pulled out his Navy Federal Credit Union Black Card, swiped it, and put it back in his credit-card holder as if it were nothing.

"I see you got the sauce, bae," he said, complimenting VerAysha on her taste in style.

"Yeah, I'm 'bout to be drippin' for you." She smiled a sexy grin.

"Both ways?" he asked.

"Yeah, bae. Both ways." For the first time, she felt herself blushing in front of him.

"Um, sir?" the clerk said.

"Yeah, what's up?" Maliss replied.

"I'm sure there's no problem but do you mind swiping your card again, please?" the sale's lady asked.

"A'ight, ain't no pressure," he said kindly. He swiped it again.

The machine beeped and alert that indicated the card had been declined.

"I'm so sorry, sir, but the machine is telling me your card is being declined for insufficient funds." The lady felt embarrassed for Maliss, though she'd never seen nor met him before. He didn't appear to be the type of man unsure of his financial situation. Something was wrong, but what, she wondered.

"What you mean *declined?*" he repeated with emphasis. This ain't no regular card, miss, this a black card. Try it again," he suggested, "there must be something wrong with your machine or somethin'." Now, he was frowning, and beyond annoyed.

"We tried it twice and it was the same result both times, sir," the clerk said.

"A'ight, you right. Try this one," he said, pulling out his Master black card. He put it in the machine and swiped it.

Again, the machine sounded off giving them the same results.

"Declined, sir." By this point, the kindness the clerk had shown a few seconds prior was slowly diminishing.

"I know that! I can fuckin' hear you know?" he said irritably. What the fuck is goin' on?" He looked at the card then the clerk.

VerAysha was nervous because she wanted all her stuff. She had nothing close to being enough to cover the costs. She stayed quiet and remained calm on the outside. On the inside she was worried and wanted to scream, *what the fuck?* She was way across the country without clean clothes and everything else. The situation was looking bad and she was beginning to feel embarrassed, but she knew there had to be a reason this was happening. I mean, after all, Maleek had just flown her on a private jet to Thailand.

Maliss tried all the cards he had in his wallet and got the same result each time—declined, declined, declined! He card had given him a zero balance. He speed-dial every one of his bank, because he was sure it had to be a mistake unless he was being punk'd. Unfortunately, each bank he contacted gave him the same answer by informing him his account had a zero balance. In addition, each representative reminded him of the "so-called transaction" he'd made earlier in the week when he'd "supposedly" transferred all his funds to an untraceable account. He threw the phone across the Gucci Store. Now, he was stuck with multimillion dollars' worth of credit to repay. Sure he had emergency bread in the cut, but not to the extent he was out.

"How the fuck is this shit possible? Millions just disappeared out my fuckin' accounts without a trace! Shit sound like the fuckin' title of a scary ass movie or some shit!" He rant and raved. "Don't worry, I'm fa'sho get to the bottom of this shit," he said. "I ain't playin' 'bout my mufuckin' bread. If I find out it's the banks' fault, I'ma own all them muthafuckas! Believe that," he said, with a scowl etched across his face.

"Sir, do we need to put these items back?" the clerk asked. She was hoping like hell he'd still be able to pay thus allowing her to receive a healthy commission from the grand sale.

"Hell nah!" he snapped. "That won't be necessary."

"How would you like to pay?" she asked curious to know if he actually had *that* much cash on him.

"I'ma pay half off my prepaid debit cards. Luckily, I keep some backup plans just in case," he said. "I'ma pay the other half off my Gucci Credit card, thanks to y'all in-house credit. This shit is crazy, bae."

He looked at VerAysha as he swiped his cards. She was so happy she got moist watching him swipe the cards. She damn near came on herself when payments from both cards was accepted. She loved a man who could plan. She would've never thought he was worth the amount of money he questioned each bank about, and it made her wonder what he *really* did for a living.

"Thank you for shopping at Gucci, please come again, sir. Please, enjoy your items," the clerk said.

"It had to be a mistake, bae," VerAysha said, rubbing his back gently, as they exited the store.

"You damn right, it's a mistake," he said. Then, he texted Hawk to see what his account was doing.

Though things had gotten off to a rocky start, nonetheless, Maliss showed VerAysha an excellent time. They went hiking, snorkeling, parasailing and hang gliding, and they even jet skied before hitting a few clubs. When the day had finally come to an end, they lodged on the top floor of the Trump Resort in the penthouse suite.

They were exhausted and the hot steaming showers they took massage every muscle of their anatomy. The fatigue nor jetlag stopped Maliss from sexing his new lady. She was surprisingly turned on when they recorded themselves. VerAysha was bent over on knees, watching their session in real-time as Maliss pounded her from the back. She was sure she'd be in love and down for almost anything after this.

Maliss was madder than a lion who had just got robbed of his meal by a pack of hyenas. He remained calm and in control for his woman because he had to show her a good time like he had planned. And, that's exactly what he did until they left.

The next day they boarded the jet. Maliss slept until they reached Atlanta, GA. He exited the jet with malice on his mind.

Paper Boi Rari

CHAPTER 27

LEHYA and SONYA
On a Mission

While Maliss was out of the country, Lehya and Sonya made sure to stay on top of the business. They had been to *Universal Spies* twice, both times ending with negative results neither of them liked. Universal Spies had too many rules and regulations to qualify for trackers and listing devices. They could have easily gone back with fake IDs, but their faces would've still been on camera. Plus, one of the requirements required using their thumb prints. Now they could've put the fake prints together also, but that wouldn't have prevented them from being recorded.

So now, they had two options—break in and steal them all, or robbery with the arm, ensuring they get the majority of the devices while also throwing extra stuff in they don't really need. By doing that, the robbery would look authentic and not as if they were out to get just the specific device—either way it had to be done.

"Damn, we gonna have to run up in that bitch and clean they ass out. We can't get our face dirty 'cause damn near the whole city would recognize us girl," Lehya said.

"Yeah, that's a bet. but you already know I'm down for the cause girl. Fuck it. Plus, Maleek basically demanded the shit and he's depending on *us*," Sonya said. "We done come too far to turn back now, so what's the plan?" she asked, as she popped another Molly

"Well, I got these right here, bitch." She showed Sonya two pair of elevated shoes. "They gonna give us the height we need to make it look like the robbers were males," she said.

The shoes came with different inches of height that could be added onto the soles, and they came in any brand you wanted. They were really made for the handicap peoples who had a leg impairment, usually one shorter than the other.

"I found them online. Last but not least, I got a couple of voice changers. I feel good about everything, and I already purchased a sports car from them Flat Head lames. They just don't know they the target. Let's turn the city up! Rain in the forecast tomorrow, bitch," Lehya said, hyped about the lick. Plus, the Molly had taken its effect on her as well.

She had just showed Sonya the voice disguise and real human disguise she'd gotten offline from a Halloween site. They had no idea that Maleek aka Maliss had a real passion for robbing and burglary, his number one occupation. They were ready, and Lehya had done her homework well. Both women had two GLOCK 40s with the 30-round clips up under them.

"Hell yeah, Lehya! This is some high-end shit," Sonya said, holding the pieces of steel up, admiring them. "I can get used to this Bonnie and Clyde shit, girl. It can be put to use on other shit to. What we gonna do with these car thief demos?"

"Maleek said, he don't care what we do wit' 'em. He just want them to feel the same way they make others feel when they stuff come up missin'. Whether it be stealin' their cars or or burnin' they shit down. Me, personally, I'm down for a little bit of it all," Lehya said.

"Me too, hoe! Me too!" Sonya agreed.

***

Maliss was back in the states with one thing on his mind, vengeance. He had finally gotten his video footage back on the incident that took place when his business, The Spot, had been purposely burned down. He found out it The Flat Head Gang was responsible. At first, he was gonna kill them all. Then, he had a better idea. He was going to find out if they could endure the same thing they dished out and see how they liked it. He had found out where their chop shop was located, but he wanted to also know where they laid their heads at night. So, he put Lehya and Sonya on them. Once everything was in place, he wanted to be updated immediately.

Anyone he suspected of playing a part in his business being burned to the ground, was responsible for his money missing. And unfortunately, they were about to find out exactly why they called him "Maliss". The bank managers would get it too if they couldn't tell him something he wanted to hear. Pain had to be inflicted to get some mouths running. Someone knew something about something, and that, he was sure of. And, he was just the man to make them want to talk.

***

9:20 a.m. the next morning, Lehya and Sonya sat in an '89 IROC z28, souped-up with a 502, and equipped with a super charger. Lehya was controlling the drone, flying it through the perimeter to see how 12, the po-po, was moving. They needed to determine the time the entire break in would take, right down to the last second, from getting in and out, to the interstate.

Sonya was on Google map keeping tabs on the traffic that was in and out of the Universal Spy Shop, parking lot. Since the rain was pouring down, there weren't many people out, so the lot was nearly empty. Due to the weather, 12 was also at a standstill.

Sonya had on the voice disguise under her real human disguise. The real human disguise was a black Rasta nigga with shoulder length dreads sporting a pair of black Ray Bans. She'd made it so her height appeared to be six two. The black Polo spring jacket with black 501s went well with the black quarter cut Timberland's she wore on her feet.

Lehya's disguise resembled Kodak-black looking nigga with a lil' webbie bob which was also paired with Ray Ban's. She stood six feet even in black 501s, Polo boots, black gloves, and a black spring Polo jacket.

"A'ight, it's show time, bitch! You ready or what?" Lehya said to Sonya.

"Yep, as ready I'll ever be," Sonya told her. "The parking lot is clear so let's ride!" Sonya was hyped and she was ready to prove her worth to Maliss. Both women were geeked off the combination of Molly and ice they'd been on all day. They had mixed the two drugs together and they were high out of their minds. And, anyone familiar with the two street drugs knew when you put the two together like that, it was referred to as Astronaut dust. They felt like they were on a rocket ship.

Lehya pulled around and slid in the parking lot.

"Right here, right here! Pull up, come on! Come on, come on," Sonya said anxiously.

"A'ight, a'ight! Calm down, bitch, let's go," Lehya said.

She pulled up in front of the door and hopped out, leaving the doors cracked. She stayed crouched down as she ran inside the building. The clerk was behind the desk with his head down, preparing to transfer the large bills from the drawer to the safe box. Suddenly, he spotted two individuals moving fast, brandishing firearms, on the monitor. The monitor was right next to him behind the counter which gave him the perfect view. He pressed the silent alarm and didn't panic. He did as he'd been trained and continued moving about as though he'd never seen them.

The clerk was a geeky looking white dude in his early thirties. He was skinny with long hippy looking hair. He knew it would take the authorities at least three to five minutes to arrive due to the weather, more like two and a half to four and a half minutes now, since he'd gotten the up's on them.

"Put yo' muthafuckin' hands where I can see 'em and step the fuck back from the counter, bitch!" Lehya's voice was deep. She pointed the forty at him.

Sonya was already on it. First, she shoved a whole shelf of trackers in her pillowcase then she ran to the listening device section. Once she found the right shelf, in one quick motion, she shoved them in the pillowcase in less than thirty-two seconds. Due to the astronaut dust, she was moving at lightening-speed. Once she finished there, she ran over to the bionic eyes section and pushed some more shit in her pillowcase.

"Move bitch! Turn around and don't fuckin' look at me!" she yelled in a stern tone. Next, Sonya jumped the counter to clear the register. As soon as she looked down, she noticed the security monitors. The red button was beeping and flashing, alerting her that the alarm had been set off. She didn't know when the clerk had set it off, so time was of the essence. "Shit! Shit! Shit! Shit! Come on, let's move," she shouted like a crazed maniac. "Now! This bitch pushed the alarm with his stupid ass!" She looked at the clerk and screamed, "Wrong move, dummy!"

BOOM! BOOM! BOOM!!

She hit the clerk three times—two in the face, one in the chest. She hopped the counter and took off right behind Sonya towards the exit.

"Come the fuck on!" Sonya said, not bothering to look back. However, Lehya had already made it to the car. By the time Sonya threw the bag in and jumped inside behind it, the police were pulling in at full speed.

Lehya put the car in reverse and hit the gas. She took off so fast, she hadn't realized Sonya's door was still open. Sonya was thrown out and went rolling across the ground.

Lehya hit the brakes, refusing to leave her girl out there like that. The police were steadily pulling in and now they had the entry blocked off. It would be nearly impossible to escape.

"Get up, girl! Come on, come on!" Lehya screamed, waving her hand for Sonya to get up.

"Mmm, ugh, agh," Sonya moaned. She tried to move but couldn't. She was hurt badly and there was three-inch gash down her inner leg. "Go, go . . . Go on and leave, Lehya. It's over for me," she managed to say.

Lehya hit the gas and the 502 shook the ground.

"Freeze!" The police shouted as he aimed his pistol directly at Lehya.

POP! POP! POP!

The police let loose on the Camaro. Lehya was so geeked up, the drugs only enhanced her concentration. She was still focused on getting away. The .40 lay across her lap as she guided the

Camaro like a Nascar race car driver. She hit three donuts then drove the car up over the curb and hit the street. Once the tire hit the asphalt, it was hard to keep up. She was moving and wanted to hit the interstate but knew she couldn't go straight to it. She hit a right causing the wheels to burn rubber, then hit a hard left, making sure the gears shifted on point. The police were slowly losing sight of the Camaro, so she hit another right hard. The Camaro slid on the rainy road, but she remained in control.

The sirens blared and the police lights whirled 'round and 'round. The blue bird was almost there. She heard it, and she had just enough time to clear it to the interstate, she was right there. *I got this*, she thought, *come on, baby, go, go, go*! She pounded the steering wheel with her hands.

Lehya hit the ramp and hit the interstate, picking up speeds of one hundred seventy-five miles per hour in just nine seconds. The 502 was made for quarter mile races anyway. They were built powerful. The one she was driving had Ultra power with a super charger on it. She had finally lost the police, but they already radioed a chopper and it was on the way. She knew her only chance was to hurry up and try to escape on feet or she would be hit. She came up on the next exit and went behind the Lenox Mall. She grabbed the pillowcase and snatched the disguise off. She quickly pulled her clothes off and threw everything in the car and set it on fire. Then, she started walking, taking big strides. Now, she was dressed in a pink halter top and some lime-green stretch pants, with some Asics Gel-Quantum 360 4 on. She came up on some apartments and went inside and sat on the stairs like she belonged there.

"Google closest Uber to Peach Tree Apartment Complex," she said into her phone.

"Closest Uber is four minutes away at Lenox Mall. Phone number is 4-0-4-6-2-9-98-35," the Google voice said.

"Call it," Lehya said.

"Calling," the Google voice said.

She waited to be picked up. Then she texted Maleek the bad news and put her head in her lap and cried for her best friend, Sonya. "Damn! Damn! Damn! Sonya," she screamed.

***

The police were done booking Sonya, but they were angry because they couldn't get a word out of her. "I want my lawyer," is all she'd said. So, they patched her up and took her to get dressed out.

"Okay, come on back here with me," the male C.O said, leading her to the laundry room. She knew it was over, but she made them do their job. The disguises were so authentic, no one could tell she was actually a female.

"Okay, strip," the C.O said. She begin dancing seductively and undoing the Polo jacket first. "Hey, homes, check it," the officer told her, "I ain't wit' no homo shit! I'll beat that downtown Atlanta shit right out yo' fuck ass, nigga! Fuck wrong wit' you? I'm from that dirty dixie! Now hurry up and take that shit off," he said. Sonya took off the jacket and her huge breasts popped out first, along with the outline of the real human disguise she was wearing. "What? What the fuck? Come over and pull that shit off," the officer demanded. Once the officer got it off of her, he was amazed at what he was seeing. Instead of the man he'd thought he arrested, a bad ass Asian bitch stood before him. He was at a lost for word's for a second. "Damn, this shit fire right here! If it was up to me, I'd let you go just for the effort you put in lil' sexy," he said.

The officer escorted her back to booking and everyone was shocked. They called homicide, and not long after, Lieutenant Jones and Sergeant Brent came over. Once again, they tried to get Sonya to talk and came up short. She was charged with first degree murder and first degree robbery. Lieutenant Jones contacted Agent Monroe and Agent Patricia at the Federal Building.

"You don't have to talk. They gonna gas chamber your lil' fine ass in the FEDS, bitch! You murdered a hard working citizen, a parent of two, a husband, a white man!" Lt. Jones said, jabbing his finger in her face.

Sonya spit in his face and Lt. Jones slapped her so hard, her head turned.

***

Lehya was at one of Maliss' houses in the city, explaining to Maliss and Hawk what happened and why. Maliss just shook and scratched his head. By now, he was beyond mad.

"So y'all out here robbin' shit now? Without consultin' wit' me? Is that what you sittin' up here tellin' me? And, on top of that, you tellin' me my baby locked up," he asked in a raised voice. He stared a hole through Lehya.

"Well, yeah, bae. We couldn't get the shit the way you asked us to. We didn't want to disappoint you, you feel me. So we did what we had to do, and shit, I hate it went like this, but all this is just part of the circumstances we live with, my love," she said. hunching her shoulders.

Maliss looked at Hawk like the bitch was crazy. Hawk shook his head because he admired her gangsta but knew all too well about cause and effect. Right now, shit was way too real right there.

"So check it. There's a body involved in a robbery with merchandise missing, and there was hi-tech equipment involved to pull it off, and now they got a suspect at large. Them muthfuckas got full man hunt goin' on out there right, lookin' for the missin' link. And I bet they offerin' a big reward. The Feds gon' put so much pressure on Sonya," he said, looking at Lehya, "she just might break."

"She's as solid as they come, so don't even doubt my bitch," Lehya responded defensively.

"Lehya, shit real right now. Do you know about the FEDS?"

"No, but I do know Sonya, and she gonna stand up in the paint! I can stamp that, love!"

"A'ight, if you say so, but only time will tell," Maliss said. Ain't shit we can do now but pray y'all 'cause me and yo' life depend on it. So, we gon' stick to the script and apply pressure on

Flat Head them. Come here. I love you, bae." He wrapped his arms tightly around Lehya.

Breaking News . . .

"Hi, this is Robin Meadows at HLN reporting live. It's a sad day for the city of Atlanta, GA. A robbery slash homicide took place at Universal Spy Shop at 9:30 a.m. this morning. The robbery resulted in the death of a store clerk—a thirty-two- year-old Caucasian male whose name has not yet been released due to further investigation. As of right now, we do know that two black males entered and robbed the store and the end result was the death of an innocent citizen.

We know that the police have one of the suspects in custody and there's still one at large. The authorities have assembled a full-fledge man hunt which is in motion as we speak. It seems they have found the car that is assumed to have been used in the crime, and apparently the getaway car. It appears that a fire was set in an effort to get rid it of any evidence," she said. Robin showed a picture in hopes that a viewer could help the police with missing clues. "Please, go ahead Agent Malone. What can you tell us about this terrible tragedy, sir?" Robin Meadows asked.

"Well, Miss Meadows, as of right now, we have the majority of our manpower on the hunt for the second suspect. We now have reason to believe the suspect is a female," Agent Malone said.

"A female? Why is that?" Robin asked.

"Well, we're not positive yet but we have strong evidence showing it could be a possibility. We've learned that our first suspect was really a female disguised as a mn. She was wearing this," —he held up the human disguise Sonya had been wearing— "So, we aren't ruling anything out. Other than that, we don't have much of a lead. The suspect in custody isn't talking yet. We have to rely on the community to help us as much as they can so we can close this case and give the victim and his family peace. Please," he pleaded, "if anyone knows anything that can help us further our investigation and arrest all parties involved, speak up!

Please, don't hesitate to call one eight hundred ANONYMOUS-TIPS. There's a reward out for thirty-five thousand dollars if the information received leads to an arrest. The suspect could be wounded considering there were over twenty bullet holes in the vehicle. So be on the lookout, and keep in mind, the suspect is armed and dangerous. That's all I have for now, Robin," Agent Malone said.

"Wow, and there you have it guys. Look at those masks," Robin said, as the camera focused on it. "Look at the number on the screen guys and call now if you know anything," Robin said.

Maliss hit the mute button. "See what I'm talkin' 'bout?" he said, pointing at the TV.

"You lucky the shots even missed you, Lehya! Twenty shots?" Hawk said, shaking his head.

"Yeah, I know, I know," she said. She got up and went to the other room to pop another Molly, to help calm her nerves.

***

Sonya was in the dorm watching the news and cursing the reporter out as if she could hear her. She picked up the phone to make a collect call. She dialed the number. "Damn, Lehya, why you hit the gas like that, bitch? That shit threw my ass right out into the wolves' mouth. I'm glad you got away though, ho," she said, talking low to herself while waiting for her call to be answered. He eyes started to water as the stress began to kick in.

"Hello?" Lehya picked up the phone wondering why the number had shown up as unavailable.

As soon the call connected, an automated voice came through the receiver:

> *You have a collect call from:*
> "Sonya."
> *Press zero to accept and accept the charges.*

Lehya hung up just as fast as she'd answered.

"What the fuck," Sonya said, looking at the phone in disbelief.

Lehya looked at Maliss. "I know this dumb bitch ain't callin' me right now! This fuckin' fast? Is she crazy? I'm changin' my shit right now," Lehya said. And without a second thought, she called her phone carrier and got her number changed.

"What?" Maliss said. He shook his head, clearly frustrated. He walked over to the bar and fixed him and Hawk a drink.

Sonya waited for a minute or two and tried to call again.

> *"The number you've reached has been changed, disconnected, or is no longer in service. Please be sure you've dialed the right number and try your call again,"* the operator said.

"Ugh, stupid bitch," Sonya mumbled. She slammed the phone down.

"Calm down, girl," a female inmate said, "trust me, I know the feeling. As soon as a bitch get on lock—"

"Know it by yourself, bitch!" Sonya said, mean mugging the inmate. She didn't bother to let the girl get the words out of mouth because she wasn't trying to make friends. "You don't know shit bout me! I'm good, and I ain't friendly, hoe! I don't wanna talk! Fuck wrong wit' you? Keep that shit to yo'self!" Sonya had snapped on the girl in a matter of minutes. Then she stomped off to her cell to lay down and pray. In that moment, *He* was the only one there to console her, then she drifted off to sleep.

CHAPTER 28

ROE BLACK
I Come B4 We

It was towards the end of the summer and Roe Black finally had luck on his side. He kept his face clean with his probation officer and he had finished the workshop for the Small Business Administration. He had his business plan finished, and his bread was up to fund it himself. Although he was applying for a loan of a hundred thousand dollars, he was going to invest it right back into the drug trade with his main man, Maliss. He was supposed to open up a wet T-shirt drive-thru car wash that offered a free vaccum from the girls. He called it *Exotic Drive-Thru.*

Hawk had just come through and dropped him off ten thousand packs of space, three thousand percs, three thousand zannies, fifteen hundred roxies, and a brick and a half of ice, which was bath salt that wouldn't show up in a urine test. The salt had the number one sales next to the space. Everything was designer drugs. If you don't know what they are, they're known on the streets as synthetics. The synthetic weed was number one. It was referred to as 'space' in my city but known as 'legal' to the world.

He finally had Troy, AL. like he'd always wanted, and he had his hometown Clio, AL. on smash! He and J-Racks were in high competition for Dothan, AL, but he'd finally reached the goal he'd longed for since the H.T.H.G. had the city. Hill Top Hustlers was old news. Now with these designer drugs, Roe Black had the keys to the city and that H.T.H.G. didn't work anymore. He had changed the locks and became the Kingpin of the city. He was swagg surfing the wave, all thanks to Maliss' blessings.

There was only one problem with his glory. When dope had a strong hold on the community, that was when it seemed to arouse suspicion with the authorities. In other words, when the dope is too strong it won't be long before the law steps in. The space was super strong and right now it was in high demand; however, it was also was a world epidemic.

All over the country they were having episodes. Episodes were when a person put on a whole show for like thirty minutes straight with no commercials. There could be just one character, or there could be multiple characters in one act. They'd become dogs, rappers, scientists, birds, fish, monsters, all kinds of shit. I even saw a nigga turn into a chainsaw one-time, real cap. They'd be literally out of their minds and nothing could stop them or bring them back except time. A person could have an episode that lasted from five minutes to thirty minutes, sometimes longer. It all depended on the potency of the product.

Then you had the synthetic ice. Ever since it hit the city there had been an increase of thefts, burglaries, and violence. Ice kept a person up for days and it enhanced a person's attitude times fifty. It was a very addictive must-have. Roe Black wasn't prepared for the kinds of side effects and episodes he was witnessing. He was at a total lost when they started taking place. He hadn't thought of how it would possibly affect him, especially since he was the one selling the drugs. He had become blinded by the money. He also made himself believe people were just exaggerating and doing all the crazy antics for attention. He had smoked space two years prior and it had never done that to him. That was then though, and this was now. Since then, the manufacturers had experimented with the chemicals on a whole other level.

His phone rang. "Yeah, what it do?" Roe Black answered.

"Shit, a bandie, you still at the hall, ain't you?" the customer said.

"Yeah, I'm in place, five racks on the money, my nigga!"

"Fa'sho. En route now. Be there in ten minutes."

"A'ight!" Roe hung up. His phone chimed again. "Yeah, what up?"

"A six pack with a baby doll to go."

"Forty-two grown men and three teenagers," Roe replied.

"Bet that, on the way," another customer said.

Another call. "Yeah?" Roe couldn't put his phone down for five minutes.

"Five and five," the caller said, "slow me down if I'm moving too fast!"

"Who this Ron?" Roe Black asked.

"Already!"

"Never too fast, shit. Speed it up, my nigga, let's see . . . A'ight, yeah two plus two equals four, partner!" Roe called out the numbers to him

"Run it then!"

"That's what it do," Roe Black said after he hung up. He was trappin' outside the pool hall off the Blvd doing big numbers. Quick flips make quick trips. He had just sent Hawk back up the highway with a cool forty-six thousand real fast. He had paid twenty thousand for the space at two dollars a pack, a dollar a pill on the percs, and a dollar a pill on the zannies. Five dollars a pill on the roxys and twelve-five for the brick and a half of the ice, an end balance totaling forty-six thousand.

A bandie was a thousand packs of space, and five racks was five thousand dollars at five dollars apiece. A six pack and a baby doll was six hundred packs of space, and four and a half ounces of ice. Forty-two grown men and three teenagers was forty-two hundred for the space, and three thousand dollars for the four and a half. Five and Five slow me down was five hundred percs and five hundred zannies. Two plus two equals four was two thousand plus two thousand equal four thousand.

He put a nick of Incredible Hulk in his weed pipe to hit when he got ready to leave. Once he collected his cash, he was going to go put his supply and cash away because he had met Hawk at the pool hall. He lit the blunt and hit it two light times and passed it around. He didn't like blunts so he fucked with the pipe, plus he had snorted a little something, so he was getting a drain at the same time.

Lt. Lawson of the Troy Police Department, and Agent Smoote of the Federal division of Drugs, Explosives, and Alcohol rode around asking question about the synthetics they had been getting so many complaints about. They had started harassing people for valuable information. When they finally got a lucky tip, they headed to the pool hall. When they got there, they saw a crowd of people pointing and laughing at someone on the ground.

"Ha, ha, ha, ughhh, you nasty, nigga," the crowd was saying.

They got out the car and walked over to see what all the excitement was about. Once they reached the crowd, they saw a man sitting Indian style eating shit out of both hands with his pants down to his knees. Next to him was a pile of vomit. A blunt roach lay next to the man. Beside it was a little baggie with a green Incredible Hulk flexing his muscles with no shirt on, cut off blue shorts, no shoes, and a pair of Versace Shades covering his eyes.

Agent Smoote bent down and picked up the pack and looked at it. Then he put it in a plastic bag. It had the words ten grams written on it.

"What the fuck?" Lt. Lawson said as he looked down at the man on the ground eating his own shit.

"Damn shame what people do for attention," Agent Smoote said. He looked at the man then at the crowd. The whole crowd was high and moving in slow motion. The detectives had just missed Roe Black.

"Where can I find some of this?" Lt. Lawson asked, trying his hand while they were under the influence. They were high but not that high, everyone started to scatter.

***

Roe Black stopped at the BP to get gassed up and to head home. He stayed off Pike Rd, twenty minutes outside of Troy, AL. and seven minutes from Murda Town Montgomery, AL. After he paid for his gas, he jumped in the whip. Today he was in his all black Cadillac XT5 on chrome and black 26-inch Forge rims. He found MoneyBagg Yo and pressed playa:

I'm on dem drugs for real/ ran off on the plug for real/
Doom! Doom! Doom! Yeah, I'm poppin pills like I'm ill.
DOOM! DOOM! DOOM!

As MoneyBagg Yo played, he grabbed his weed pipe, lit it up, hit the whole bowl hard, and pulled off. He looked at the pipe for a split second as he eased into traffic. His eyes got big and he dropped the pipe and grabbed the steering wheel with both hands. He was still inhaling it when he stopped at the red light. He knew he had fucked up, but it was too late. He was juggin' at the light to the music like he was good. He had already started sweating profusely. The light was still red, and he finally blew the smoke out. As soon as he did, he instantly transformed and hit the gas, running through the red light.

He begin to howl like a werewolf as sweat poured down his face. People in the cars behind him blared their car horns. Then cars started crashing all around him.

"Argh!" he screamed out and beat the steering wheel at the same time. "Vroom, vroom," he said out loud, making race car sounds now. He had turn into a race car driver in his mind. He was in and out of traffic weaving. He must've known where he was going because he had made it through the city unnoticed. At least unnoticed by the law. He turned onto Pike Rd. and flew by a state trooper doing a hundred one miles per hour.

The state trooper hit the lights and got in hot pursuit.

"Vroom, vroom," Roe Black shouted. No need to speed bitches this my win," he shouted, zoned out.

"Black Cadillac XT5 SUV reaching speeds of over a hundred miles per hour, and still seems to be excelling on Pike Rd. In hot pursuit, send back up." The state trooper radioed for assistance. Next, he called in to dispatch. "Calling all cars! Calling all cars, hot pursuit on Pike Rd! Black Cadillac XT5," the dispatch called repeated and called out to all cars listening.

"A little more action for you to get out here, Agent Smoote. Let's see what we got?" Lt. Lawson said, as he headed towards Pike Rd.

The state trooper caught up with the SUV but couldn't stop it. Roe Black was still out of his mind with the pedal to the metal. By the time he came back around, he was in Montgomery, AL. He had by passed his house a long time ago. Once he realized what was taking place, it was way too late. He knew he was fucked and started thinking of a plan within a plan—a plan he had made a long time ago just in case one of these moments ever presented itself.

He had been doing so good that he still hadn't spent the bank robbery money. Right now, he had cash money, drugs, and a GLOCK 40 with the thirty-round magazine in it, all on the back seat, plus the pipe was on the floor. The GLOCK happened to be the same exact one he and Maliss had used in the bank robbery, and he still had the phone he'd silenced when Maliss told him to turn it off.

Roe Black knew all too well what all this meant. If he was charged with a 924.C it would be starting at five years for the gun being with the drugs, and that was with or without felonies. Aside from that, was the extended clip, and add to all of that two more consecutive sentences for the drugs and money that would run consecutively. Consecutive sentences meant he couldn't start on the new sentence until the one he would be doing at the current time had run its course. Once he finished that one, only then would the next one start to be counted for a 924.C, a charge that consisted of either robbery with a gun, or drugs and a gun, or a gun with a large sum of currency. Basically, according to the law it meant he was protecting the drugs and money or putting others in danger by taking something.

"Fuck, fuck, fuck! Man damn this shit! Fuck you! Not like this, Lord! PLEASE," Roe Black said, beating on the steering wheel. It was way too late for prayer though. Everything was unfolding slowly. He was a low life nigga though. He couldn't take it by himself. He blamed the next nigga and was determined to get his man by all means. He pulled over and kept his hands on the steering wheel.

"Freeze! Put your hands where I can see 'em now," the state trooper yelled, ordering him. He pointed his gun as he ran up on the SUV. When he was on him, he snatched him out and cuffed him in record-breaking time.

Lt. Lawson and Agent Smoote pulled up just as the state trooper was putting Roe Black in the backseat of the patrol car. Lt. Lawson was out of his authority, but he would still get some of the action because it had initially started in his county.

Agent Smoote walked over to SUV and started searching it. "jack pot," he shouted out to the state trooper, as he pulled out the drugs, gun, and money, and held it up.

The state trooper looked then whistled shaking his head. "Yeah, jackpot," he said, as he walked to the SUV.

"Book 'em Dano!" Lt. Lawson said, smiling. They all looked at Roe Black and shook their heads as several more patrol cars pulled up.

Roe Black dropped his head. If this didn't work, he was through. He'd spend at least five hundred and forty months of his life in the United States Federal Prison. Plus, he would have another consecutive violation to serve too, because he was still on supervised release, he thought to himself.

Montgomery, AL. Federal Building

Roe Black was sitting in the investigation room waiting nervously for to be interrogated. He had gone over his plan for the umpteenth time. He had only been there for twenty-five minutes but to him it felt more like five hours had already gone by.

Time in solitary seemed to have that effect on a person. This was a game that the law loved to play on the opts, the individuals they chose to single out. They understood in order to conquer and destroy, you had to first divide, sit back and watch it all fall. What else other than solitude to pull it off. In less than thirty minutes, they watched him through the one-way mirror as he started to fall apart. Roe Black's legs shook up and down violently. Though that could've been due to the fact that it was freezing in the little room.

The temperature felt like it was below zero. He had also begun to talk to himself as if he were reading or rehearsing a script.

Agent Smoote walked in carrying a clip board and a recorder. Behind him was another agent Roe hadn't seen earlier, along with Lt. Lawson. They gave Roe Black two options . . . tell or jail!

"A'ight. Mr. Smith, what's it gonna be? What you got for us?" Agent Smoote said smugly. He made himself comfortable and sat across the table from Roe. He turned the recorder on and passed Roe Black a Simply Orange brand container of juice. "Here. It might be the last free world drink you get to taste for the rest of your life."

"Well, what y'all gon' do for me if I help?" Roe Black asked. He reached for the juice.

"If it's good enough you might miss jail today," Smoote said.

"I want it in writing. I ain't no fool now! Plus, my lawyer here too," he said. Opening his drink to take a sip.

"Well, if it's like that then this must be good! Better not be a waste of our time or I'll see to it you die in prison, Mr. Smith, understood?"

"It's so good you gon' end up bein' in charge of yo' whole division, Agent Smoote. So, yeah, understood," he said.

What they, nor Maliss knew, was that Roe had been an informer before. He'd told on his first federal case and got a time cut. Thirty minutes later, his lawyer arrived and, he signed the contract. By the time he had finished, they were damn near ready to give him a suit, office, and a badge. He had given up everything he could muster up out of his mental rolodex.

The first thing he gave them was the info about Hawk being on the highway with a substantial amount of money. He informed them that he'd just spent the same money on the product they had just confiscated from the SUV. By telling them that bit of information he had already gained leverage on them.

***

Maliss had tried over and over to call Roe Black to see how he liked his new demo. He also wanted to check in on him, but he kept getting his voicemail. He hung up and started to hit Hawk up, but he was also trying to walk down his money and figure out who was responsible for it. He was waiting on some help to come by since he had hired someone to check on his situation. He had no idea of the danger that was coming to him, from all angles, at one time. The robbers were in motion, plus the rats were working against him too. Let's not forget the scorned baby-mama drama. He didn't know what to suspect because as far as he knew, there were no snitches, rats, or snakes in his camp.

"Damn, why the fuck this nigga phone off? All this money to be made. He must be puttin' his shit up before he come back to jugg. That's right, young nigga! They on your time. Don't rush into nothin'. That's how you win!" Maliss said, as he pulled up at his trap on the southside on Atlanta, GA.

***

Roe Black was finishing his orange juice and ready to give his statement. He signed the Proffer Agreement letter and agreed to continue with the interview. He provided the following information, concerning the drugs and his role in the bank robbery in Auburn Bank on April 29, 2020. He didn't know where Maliss stayed exactly and he didn't have exact times on when he would cop his drugs. So, he told more about the robbery with the promise to try and score from him as long as they let him walk free.

The Proffer Agreement read like this:

Rasheed J. Smith, that of birthday June 29, 1989, social security account number. It was blacked out. Then it continued:

He was interviewed under a Proffer Agreement at the United States Federal Building, middle District of Alabama, Montgomery, Alabama. Also present during the interview were Assistant United States Attorney (AUSA) John Steel, Federal De'bouter Don Ben Becks, Bureau of

Drugs, Explosives, and Alcohol. (DEA) Special Agent Smoote, (SA), Time Vander, and (TPD) Lt. Lawson.

Prior to the interview, Smith was provided a copy of the Proffer Agreement letter and was afforded the opportunity to speak to his attorney.

Smith met Maliss in prison in Talladega, Alabama. Maliss told Smith they were going to get real money together once they got out. He knew of all kinds of ways to get it.

After being released, both Smith and Maliss were at the halfway house at the same time. Smith in Montgomery, Maliss in Atlanta.

Maliss called Smith and devised a plan while they were in the halfway house, on the weekend before the robbery. Maliss was to pick Smith up Monday at a gas station on Court St.

The plan was to rob the bank in Auburn Monday morning. He came in a blue mustang. They drove to Auburn. They got dressed down the street and drove back to the bank.

Upon entering the bank, Roe Black recalled a black guy at the counter. Roe Black said he'd told the people no one would get hurt they just wanted the money. Maliss asked the employees where the safe was located. A female opened the safe, and the money was placed in a white pillowcase. After filling the pillowcase, both Smith and Maliss fled the bank in the Mustang.

Maliss told Smith to turn his phone off but he didn't, instead, Smith put it on silent. This was to keep them from being tracked. Maliss took the battery out of his.

They returned to Montgomery. They split two hundred thousand plus in cash behind the church at his baby mama's house off Fairview. Maliss dropped him off at Krystal's on Court St. before he went back to Atlanta to the halfway house he was staying in, Smith believed.

During the robbery, Maliss wore a Bob Marley hat with and black tee shirt around his face. While Smith wore a black tee around his face without the hat. Maliss provided everything.

Roe Black spent money on cars, stereo equipment, rims, giving money away, drugs and partying. He claims he doesn't have any more money left.

On the way to the bank, Maliss claimed he had been watching the bank for over ten years. He knew it would be an easy lick for them. Maliss had it planned to a tee. He even said he knew it would rain that day. He also knew the police could only drive so fast in the rain. Roe

Black stated they did not have a lookout person as the robbery took place.

Roe Black stated his statement was true, and he signed and dated it.

Rasheed Smith

7/21/20

Three and a half hours later, Roe Black was out of the Federal Building with his phone tapped, and a whole lot of marked money for the drugs he'd just bought so he could purchase more. He had set up the under play for the over play. Roe Black was about to reveal the fuck shit like the fuck nigga he was. He was about to do the Al-PO.

"Whew! Shit, that Incredible Hulk is damn sho' the strong man himself. Now look, I'm in a fucked-up position by fuckin' wit' it! My dad told me a long time ago: *The letter I comes way before U or We.* Now ain't that the truth, old man if you ever told it?" Roe Black said.

He jumped in his truck and turned his phone back on. He was back in motion without anyone knowing what had happened. He was about to sink the streets, starting with Maliss and Hawk, and so on. He didn't care who had to shit on, as long as he saved his self. He pulled into traffic and turned his music up and let the lyrics blast through:

It ain't snitchin' if you ain't suspected of it /
I'm the biggest kingpin Alabama has ever seen /
ain't nobody gon' stop my dreams!

To Be Continued...
Kingpin Dreams 3
Coming Soon

Submission Guideline

Submit the first three chapters of your completed manuscript to ldpsubmissions@gmail.com, subject line: Your book's title. The manuscript must be in a .doc file and sent as an attachment. Document should be in Times New Roman, double spaced and in size 12 font. Also, provide your synopsis and full contact information. If sending multiple submissions, they must each be in a separate email.

Have a story but no way to send it electronically? You can still submit to LDP/Ca$h Presents. Send in the first three chapters, written or typed, of your completed manuscript to:

LDP: Submissions Dept
Po Box 944
Stockbridge, Ga 30281

DO NOT send original manuscript. Must be a duplicate.

Provide your synopsis and a cover letter containing your full contact information.

Thanks for considering LDP and Ca$h Presents.

Kingpin Dreams 2

Coming Soon from Lock Down Publications/Ca$h Presents

BOW DOWN TO MY GANGSTA

By **Ca$h**

TORN BETWEEN TWO

By **Coffee**

THE STREETS STAINED MY SOUL **II**

By **Marcellus Allen**

BLOOD OF A BOSS **VI**

SHADOWS OF THE GAME II

By **Askari**

LOYAL TO THE GAME **IV**

By **T.J. & Jelissa**

A DOPEBOY'S PRAYER **II**

By **Eddie "Wolf" Lee**

IF LOVING YOU IS WRONG... **III**

By **Jelissa**

TRUE SAVAGE **VII**

MIDNIGHT CARTEL III

DOPE BOY MAGIC IV

By **Chris Green**

BLAST FOR ME **III**

A SAVAGE DOPEBOY III

CUTTHROAT MAFIA II

By **Ghost**

A HUSTLER'S DECEIT III

KILL ZONE **II**

BAE BELONGS TO ME III

A DOPE BOY'S QUEEN II

By **Aryanna**

Paper Boi Rari

CHAINED TO THE STREETS III

By **J-Blunt**

COKE KINGS V

KING OF THE TRAP II

By **T.J. Edwards**

GORILLAZ IN THE BAY V

TEARS OF A GANGSTA II

De'Kari

THE STREETS ARE CALLING II

Duquie Wilson

KINGPIN KILLAZ IV

STREET KINGS III

PAID IN BLOOD III

CARTEL KILLAZ IV

DOPE GODS II

Hood Rich

SINS OF A HUSTLA II

ASAD

TRIGGADALE III

Elijah R. Freeman

KINGZ OF THE GAME V

Playa Ray

SLAUGHTER GANG IV

RUTHLESS HEART IV

By Willie Slaughter

THE HEART OF A SAVAGE III

By Jibril Williams

FUK SHYT II

By Blakk Diamond

THE REALEST KILLAS

Kingpin Dreams 2

By Tranay Adams

TRAP GOD II

By Troublesome

YAYO III

A SHOOTER'S AMBITION III

By S. Allen

GHOST MOB

Stilloan Robinson

KINGPIN DREAMS III

By Paper Boi Rari

CREAM

By Yolanda Moore

SON OF A DOPE FIEND II

By Renta

FOREVER GANGSTA II

GLOCKS ON SATIN SHEETS II

By Adrian Dulan

LOYALTY AIN'T PROMISED II

By Keith Williams

THE PRICE YOU PAY FOR LOVE II

DOPE GIRL MAGIC III

By Destiny Skai

CONFESSIONS OF A GANGSTA II

By Nicholas Lock

I'M NOTHING WITHOUT HIS LOVE II

By Monet Dragun

CAUGHT UP IN THE LIFE III

By Robert Baptiste

NEW TO THE GAME III

By **Malik D. Rice**

Paper Boi Rari

LIFE OF A SAVAGE III

By **Romell Tukes**

QUIET MONEY II

By **Trai'Quan**

THE STREETS MADE ME II

By **Larry D. Wright**

THE ULTIMATE SACRIFICE VI

IF YOU CROSSM ME ONCE II

By **Anthony Fields**

THE LIFE OF A HOOD STAR

By Ca$h & Rashia Wilson

Available Now

RESTRAINING ORDER **I & II**

By **CA$H & Coffee**

LOVE KNOWS NO BOUNDARIES **I II & III**

By **Coffee**

RAISED AS A GOON I, II, III & IV

BRED BY THE SLUMS I, II, III

BLAST FOR ME I & II

ROTTEN TO THE CORE I II III

A BRONX TALE I, II, III

DUFFEL BAG CARTEL I II III IV

HEARTLESS GOON I II III IV

A SAVAGE DOPEBOY I II

HEARTLESS GOON I II III

DRUG LORDS I II III

Kingpin Dreams 2

CUTTHROAT MAFIA

By **Ghost**

LAY IT DOWN **I & II**

LAST OF A DYING BREED

BLOOD STAINS OF A SHOTTA I & II III

By **Jamaica**

LOYAL TO THE GAME I II III

LIFE OF SIN I, II III

By **TJ & Jelissa**

BLOODY COMMAS I & II

SKI MASK CARTEL I II & III

KING OF NEW YORK I II,III IV V

RISE TO POWER I II III

COKE KINGS I II III IV

BORN HEARTLESS I II III IV

KING OF THE TRAP

By **T.J. Edwards**

IF LOVING HIM IS WRONG…I & II

LOVE ME EVEN WHEN IT HURTS I II III

By **Jelissa**

WHEN THE STREETS CLAP BACK I & II III

THE HEART OF A SAVAGE I II

By **Jibril Williams**

A DISTINGUISHED THUG STOLE MY HEART I II & III

LOVE SHOULDN'T HURT I II III IV

RENEGADE BOYS I II III IV

PAID IN KARMA I II III

By **Meesha**

A GANGSTER'S CODE I &, II III

A GANGSTER'S SYN I II III

Paper Boi Rari

THE SAVAGE LIFE I II III
CHAINED TO THE STREETS I II
By J-Blunt
PUSH IT TO THE LIMIT
By **Bre' Hayes**
BLOOD OF A BOSS **I, II, III, IV, V**
SHADOWS OF THE GAME
By **Askari**
THE STREETS BLEED MURDER **I, II & III**
THE HEART OF A GANGSTA I II& III
By **Jerry Jackson**
CUM FOR ME I II III IV V
An **LDP Erotica Collaboration**
BRIDE OF A HUSTLA **I II & II**
THE FETTI GIRLS **I, II& III**
CORRUPTED BY A GANGSTA I, II III, IV
BLINDED BY HIS LOVE
THE PRICE YOU PAY FOR LOVE
DOPE GIRL MAGIC I II
By **Destiny Skai**
WHEN A GOOD GIRL GOES BAD
By **Adrienne**
THE COST OF LOYALTY I II III
By Kweli
A GANGSTER'S REVENGE **I II III & IV**
THE BOSS MAN'S DAUGHTERS I II III IV V
A SAVAGE LOVE **I & II**
BAE BELONGS TO ME I II
A HUSTLER'S DECEIT I, II, III
WHAT BAD BITCHES DO I, II, III

Kingpin Dreams 2

SOUL OF A MONSTER I II III

KILL ZONE

A DOPE BOY'S QUEEN

By **Aryanna**

A KINGPIN'S AMBITON

A KINGPIN'S AMBITION **II**

I MURDER FOR THE DOUGH

By **Ambitious**

TRUE SAVAGE I II III IV V VI

DOPE BOY MAGIC I, II, III

MIDNIGHT CARTEL I II

By **Chris Green**

A DOPEBOY'S PRAYER

By **Eddie "Wolf" Lee**

THE KING CARTEL **I, II & III**

By **Frank Gresham**

THESE NIGGAS AIN'T LOYAL **I, II & III**

By **Nikki Tee**

GANGSTA SHYT **I II &III**

By **CATO**

THE ULTIMATE BETRAYAL

By **Phoenix**

BOSS'N UP **I , II & III**

By **Royal Nicole**

I LOVE YOU TO DEATH

By Destiny J

I RIDE FOR MY HITTA

I STILL RIDE FOR MY HITTA

By **Misty Holt**

LOVE & CHASIN' PAPER

Paper Boi Rari

By **Qay Crockett**
TO DIE IN VAIN
SINS OF A HUSTLA
By **ASAD**
BROOKLYN HUSTLAZ
By **Boogsy Morina**
BROOKLYN ON LOCK I & II
By **Sonovia**
GANGSTA CITY
By **Teddy Duke**
A DRUG KING AND HIS DIAMOND I & II III
A DOPEMAN'S RICHES
HER MAN, MINE'S TOO I, II
CASH MONEY HO'S
By Nicole Goosby
TRAPHOUSE KING **I II & III**
KINGPIN KILLAZ I II III
STREET KINGS I II
PAID IN BLOOD **I II**
CARTEL KILLAZ I II III
DOPE GODS
By **Hood Rich**
LIPSTICK KILLAH **I, II, III**
CRIME OF PASSION I II & III
By **Mimi**
STEADY MOBBN' **I, II, III**
THE STREETS STAINED MY SOUL
By **Marcellus Allen**
WHO SHOT YA **I, II, III**
SON OF A DOPE FIEND

Kingpin Dreams 2

Renta
GORILLAZ IN THE BAY **I II III IV**
TEARS OF A GANGSTA
DE'KARI
TRIGGADALE I II
Elijah R. Freeman
GOD BLESS THE TRAPPERS I, II, III
THESE SCANDALOUS STREETS I, II, III
FEAR MY GANGSTA I, II, III
THESE STREETS DON'T LOVE NOBODY I, II
BURY ME A G I, II, III, IV, V
A GANGSTA'S EMPIRE I, II, III, IV
THE DOPEMAN'S BODYGAURD I II
Tranay Adams
THE STREETS ARE CALLING
Duquie Wilson
MARRIED TO A BOSS... I II III
By Destiny Skai & Chris Green
KINGZ OF THE GAME I II III IV
Playa Ray
SLAUGHTER GANG I II III
RUTHLESS HEART I II III
By Willie Slaughter
FUK SHYT
By Blakk Diamond
DON'T F#CK WITH MY HEART I II
By Linnea
ADDICTED TO THE DRAMA I II III
By Jamila
YAYO I II

Paper Boi Rari

A SHOOTER'S AMBITION I II

By S. Allen

TRAP GOD

By Troublesome

FOREVER GANGSTA

GLOCKS ON SATIN SHEETS

By Adrian Dulan

TOE TAGZ I II III

By Ah'Million

KINGPIN DREAMS I II

By Paper Boi Rari

CONFESSIONS OF A GANGSTA

By Nicholas Lock

I'M NOTHING WITHOUT HIS LOVE

By Monet Dragun

CAUGHT UP IN THE LIFE I II

By Robert Baptiste

NEW TO THE GAME I II

By **Malik D. Rice**

Life of a Savage I II

By **Romell Tukes**

LOYALTY AIN'T PROMISED

By Keith Williams

Quiet Money

By **Trai'Quan**

THE STREETS MADE ME

By **Larry D. Wright**

THE ULTIMATE SACRIFICE I, II, III, IV, V

KHADIFI

IF YOU CROSS ME ONCE

Kingpin Dreams 2

By **Anthony Fields**

THE LIFE OF A HOOD STAR

By Ca$h & Rashia Wilson

<ins>BOOKS BY LDP'S CEO, CA$H</ins>

<ins>TRUST IN NO MAN</ins>

<ins>TRUST IN NO MAN 2</ins>

<ins>TRUST IN NO MAN 3</ins>

<ins>BONDED BY BLOOD</ins>

<ins>SHORTY GOT A THUG</ins>

<ins>THUGS CRY</ins>

<ins>THUGS CRY 2</ins>

<ins>THUGS CRY 3</ins>

<ins>TRUST NO BITCH</ins>

<ins>TRUST NO BITCH 2</ins>

<ins>TRUST NO BITCH 3</ins>

<ins>TIL MY CASKET DROPS</ins>

<ins>RESTRAINING ORDER</ins>

<ins>RESTRAINING ORDER 2</ins>

<ins>IN LOVE WITH A CONVICT</ins>

<ins>LIFE OF A HOOD STAR</ins>

<ins>Coming Soon</ins>

BONDED BY BLOOD 2

BOW DOWN TO MY GANGSTA